CONTENTS

DISCLAIMER	1
Copyright	2
Bio	3
Dedication	5
Title Page	7
FML	8
War! What is it good for?	13
The Futurists	19
Amy	27
The Pit	33
Fuck'N'Fight	40
Another Day in Paradise	49
Showbiz	59
Food for Thought	68
The Dick	76
The Agency	82
Best Laid Plans	92
Paris Je T'aime	99
Season Finale	109
Mom and Pops	123
Iron Rick	128

Solus Tour	138
Moonland	149
The Plot Thickens	155
Moongirl	163
Third Time Lucky	171
Brock Motherfuckin' Dynamite	177
Afterword	187

DISCLAIMER

This is a work of fiction. Names, characters, places, and incidents either are the products of the author's imagination or are used fictitiously. Any resemblance to actual persons, living or dead, businesses, companies, events, or locales is entirely coincidental.

The Last Human?
By T.F.R. LeBoomington

Book 1
The Last Human Saga
By T.F.R. LeBoomington

Editor
DLP
Doctor in Nanotechnology

Cover by T.F.R. LeBoomington

ISBN: 9781796446036

www.thelasthuman.co

© 2019 T.F.R. LeBoomington

All rights reserved. This book or any portion thereof may not be reproduced or used in any manner whatsoever without the express written permission of the publisher except for the use of brief quotations in a book review.

For permissions contact:
leboomington@gmail.com

Join the conversation here!
https://www.thelasthuman.co/blog

BIO

T.F.R. LeBoomington resides between London and France. When he's not working on some mad project he's out researching his books and studying humans in their natural drinking environments.

Throughout the years he's worked in marketing, video production, gaming, smart homes and more. His passion for technology and knowledge of the tech industry is excessive and a bit geeky.

He's been writing since he was a kid, but never attempted to publish anything until 10 years ago when he tried and failed miserably. A couple of years ago he decided to start writing again, on the side. The result is The Last Human Saga. It's a product of his love of 80s and 90s pop culture mixed with his love of futurism and science-fiction, filtered through his life experience.

I dedicate this work,

To my great uncle. He died on the day I finished writing Book 2. At least I got to tell him the whole saga, he knew more than any of you reading it!

And to my family, my inspirational hardworking sisters, my mother who always believed in me whatever foolish project I pursued and my father who probably wishes I'd just get a normal job.

And to my editor, outstanding scientist and talented artist, without whom this book would the ramblings of a madman.

And to my number one fan who's managed to make me believe this is a good read. Then again she thought that on the first draft.

And to all my friends, for their support, inspiration and good times!

Thank you all so much!

THE LAST HUMAN?

BOOK ONE

By T.F.R. LeBoomington

FML

Rick could barely see. He knew there was a gun in his hand, but it kept moving in and out of focus. There was something wet in his other hand. Something hard. Something sharp. He emerged from his blackout episode standing naked in a park. Rick got the ominous feeling that, yet again, he'd fucked up. He could taste blood in his mouth. His left hand was bleeding; it was holding some sort of broken vase. He brought the flower pot to his face and smelt it. He confirmed that this receptacle did, in fact, contain booze. He took a swig. *Not bad. Fruity*. Rick blinked. He was in his living room now, or at least he hoped it was his living room. He was still naked. The gun was still in his right hand. His left hand was no longer bloody, and the broken booze vase was gone. Instead, his bandaged hand held some sort of bubble with brown liquid in it. He put in his mouth. He winced. He coughed. It went through his nose. It burnt as it did so. Whiskey. Rick looked at the gun again and thought *fuck it*. He brought the weapon up to his temple and closed his eyes. *Enough of this fuckery.* He would have pulled the trigger, but he fell asleep like that.

The first thing Rick felt when he woke up was shame. Shame at getting blackout drunk, shame at probably making a fool of himself, shame at not remembering, shame at not making it into bed, shame at waking up with a gun in his hand, shame at not having the balls to pull the trigger. The second thing he felt was pain, just good old physical pain. *Just another glorious day waiting to unfold.* From the room next door, he heard Amy telling him to get ready. Doctor's appointment.

Doctor Fuckface stared at Rick quietly, they'd been like this for a few minutes, and he hadn't said a word beyond "have a seat". The office was your typical psychiatrist office, degrees framed and mounted on the wall, couches and seats of various comfort levels and lots of books; probably just decoration, not a lot of people read these days. No need for it. The doc had bionic eyes, Rick could tell. That could only mean one thing, he was being analysed. His micro expressions measured, quantified and meaning assigned to his behaviour. Rick didn't want to be here, and Dr Freud, or whatever his name was, didn't seem to care too much. He was getting paid either way.

"So, Mr Archer, do you want to tell me a bit about yourself?" *Ah, it speaks!* "I think that would be a good start. Don't you?" *Me walking out and being done with this nonsense would be a good start.* Rick was not in the mood for sharing today, or any day unless he was drunk. *Maybe I should try this drunk next time.*

"Rick is fine." Rick waited for a nod and started again. "You know me" Rick continued, "everybody knows me, I'm fucking Rick Archer, my life is public domain..." He let out a tired sigh and looked out the window, "and it's been this way since the war ended. What do you want from me?"

"I want to help you feel better" The doc started...

Fuck you. Rick thought it, but he must have also said it because there was an awkward silence. Rick was the last non-modified human. He couldn't even get standard medical procedures. Everyone got the essential lung upgrade for free, but not Rick. No, Rick's contract forbade any type of modifications, until death. So, he was the only one walking around with a breathing mask, just one of the many things that sucked about not being a cyborg superhuman. That was fine in the beginning when he was young, and everybody died, but life could be so much more now. Limits had been pulverised. He could live forever now. In some form or other.

"My agent is forcing me to come here. Help me get back

in the zone, so I play ball. But I don't wanna play ball. I've had fucking enough of being paraded around like a fucking show monkey."

"Is that how you feel? A show monkey?"

"Listen, there's only one thing that'll make me feel better, and I'm here because you have to convince me that I could be happy some other way. I know how this shit works. I may not be some super-mutant-cyborg-genius, but I am not a fool. So, fuck you for even trying to shrink me."

Rick believed anyone who was honest with themselves and capable of introspection could identify their own psychosis and handle it. Like most in his position he was blinded to his crippling issues and those of others. His psychosis was far from under control. While true that the many brain upgrades and accompanying societal improvements had brought people to a pretty good place; the carousel of misery still went round and round, and people still rode it. Rick just thought he was the only one.

For most, mental problems and their solutions were the domain of cyber-surgeons and counter-hacking professionals, or brain geneticists. Most brain issues, all medical problems really, were solved by scanning the problem and then agreeing nanobots could fix it, then programming the nanobots to fix the issues. And those who could afford it had permanent nanobot colonies living inside of them; keeping their bodies young and healthy a while longer. Not Rick though, Rick got none of that.

"I'm only trying to do my job. I want to help." The doc seemed sincere enough, but that was beside the point. His job was to make Rick accept something he didn't want to. He could be stubborn.

"Yeah, your job… Which consists of medicating me so that I behave myself and don't have any more breakdowns live for the whole world to enjoy." The breakdowns actually made great TV, Rick knew that because his agent had told him so a hundred times. They reinforced the whole idea that simple humans were foolish beings. "So, what? Want me to tell you about my life? So you can make your little notes? Then give your advice and prescriptions? I'm pretty open with myself, and I'm already self-medicating, don't you follow the news?" Rick loved to drink, and get fucked up. It's what made life bearable. If only they'd let him get the Liver 5000 upgrade. *Goodbye hangovers.*

The doc was unfazed "That would be good, maybe tell me about your life before the cameras." Rick sighed, *might as well get this shit over with.*

"I hate my life", Rick let that sink in for a moment. It was a rare thing nowadays. He was part of that small percentage of people that still weren't happy. The Great Purge had pretty much wiped out greed and misery and the people that propagated those traits. But some moody dicks remained, and Rick was one of them.

"Hmmm, but you are rich and famous. People dream of being rich and famous."

"Yeah? Maybe they do. But I don't think anybody on this planet would want to switch places with me. Wait, bar that. I don't think anyone in Solus or any other system for that matter would want to swap with me. Would you like to have my life?" Rick let the silence last for close to a minute then muttered: "didn't think so."

The doc waited a bit longer in case Rick had more snide comments in store. Satisfied Rick was done he started again. "I want to understand you. Help me help you. Tell me about the real you. Tell me about your life with your father. Tell me about your childhood."

Rick turned away and gazed out the window wistfully. It was a grey day, a rainy day, a depressing day, a good day to get blackout drunk. That prospect cheered Rick up just enough to cooperate. For a bit.

"Fine, I'll tell you about my life. Pretty sure this shit's been covered in some documentary or two... But since you don't watch TV, follow the news or look at the internet... I'll recap everything for you." Rick was visibly disappointed that his sarcasm had not elicited a response from the doc.

"That would be great, thank you." And there it was, the smallest smile, but it was there. And that's all Rick needed, acknowledgement that he was funny.

Rick had told his story a million times. Though it wasn't just his story, it was very much his father's story. *Frank Archer the fucking hero*. People always wanted to know about the great Frank Archer and what it was like growing up with him. And Rick told them. *Though,* Rick thought, *usually I'm the one gets paid...*

WAR! WHAT IS IT GOOD FOR?

Rick Archer was born in 2016. It was a terrible year, his father had told him often. Frank lived in London then. He worked in IT for some doomed-to-fail-start-up. That year was the first year he started believing the world was going to implode. Lots of terrible decisions were made, and many great people died, but really it was just the logical continuation of their civilisation's trajectory. Frank had observed it; everyone had observed it. It's what people talked about at dinners and drinks for decades. Nations were turning inward, and fascist tendencies were resurfacing. Paranoid countries plagued by terrorism and the media fear factory were becoming police states. Politicians were suppressing the truth and stealing from the people. *Good times*.

Frank hadn't planned on having Rick, or any children for that matter. Rick had been reminded of that as often as he'd questioned his father's parenting. His mother was the most beautiful-perfect-person in the world, and she'd wanted to keep the baby. She was boss. Frank had become a father as division and mistrust spread across the globe. Old alliances failed, and the acceptance of impending doom propagated.

The world-wide generational tug-of-war gradually escalated. Frank wrote about it in his political slash conspiracy's blog. His headlines were catchy, and he had a small following. He wrote about the power and control of the industrial elite at odds with the growing tech elite. Frank was obsessed with the rise of technology and creative destruction of the old world. Especially the idea that everything would be free and robots would do all the bitch-work. He warned that the only thing that could save the old world and its greedy ways was a war. *A nice big war would do the trick.*

"Yes, yes, I know our history, Mr Archer..." Rick did not appreciate being cut off.

"Listen, you, interrupting people is rude! Now I'm telling the story, and you're listening". The doc nodded. A nod that said, "fine carry on". "Now, where was I? Oh yeah, clusterfuck in the UK prompted my parents to leave their home in London for my mother's sunny homeland. We moved to Barcelona and knowing what came after it was a good move." There was a bit of silence, the doc, like most, had lost people, and this session was going to bring some memories back. Rick continued with his story anyway.

Back then Rick's parents, like many others, were social media warriors. This consisted of signing petitions and getting people to sign petitions, and the occasional donation or marathon run challenge. Millions of people did this, and it applied slight pressure on corporations and governments, and it worked to some extent. More importantly, it empowered people, putting them in a state of mind where they believed the world could be changed to a better place, that their voice mattered. Every day these dormant rebels inched closer to the tipping point. Frank desperately tried to get the people to rage against the machine. They did not rage in time.

The war started after the collapse of NATO. A lot of madness happened after that. Even CNN struggled to keep up. The beasts of the Pacific once more fed on the bloated corpses of the young. The Middle East and Americas erupted into an orgy of chaos. And in response to the US and Turkey's departure from NATO, the European Defence Force was created. It's around that time that Britain stopped its Brexit nonsense. *Just couldn't stay out of such a nice army.* Rick paused and turned to the doctor.

"Hey doc, don't mean to pry, but it's hard to tell how old people actually are now... And from your accent, it's clear you're English..."

"Come out with it already."

"Were you in Britain during the war?"

"Yes." One word answers always sent a clear message. Rick got back to his story, the good doctor was paid to listen, and he could use the money to get help for whatever demons haunted him.

"OK, well, I'm carrying on." Still, he waited for the doc's nod. "Back home my parents, like everyone else, watched as skirmishes started between the EDF and Russian paramilitaries."

"Yes, we all know that to be lies."

"What?"

"Those soldiers were Russian military!"

"Hmmm, okay..." Rick wasn't so sure. Every Russian he'd met was crazy enough to start a war. The doc cleared his throat, bringing Rick back from his reveries. "So, things were equally terrible in Turkey. The Turkish leader had been busy making himself king and his people rebelled." Rick glanced at the doc. *No objections?*

It was time to leave Europe. Frank had published articles researching escape routes to safe havens. More of a gag at first, he'd use them for his family. His research had identified New Zealand and Chile as of the two safest places to ride out the war. The conflict was spreading to every corner of the world. It was probably already too late to make it to New Zealand. They would have to move fast, and it would have to be to Chile, and so young Rick and his parents embarked on a flight to South America.

They never made it, their plane was hijacked and crash-landed in the Canary Islands. Rick's mother died in the crash. After that Frank went a bit mental, mostly mumbling about a revenge spree of sorts. First, though, he grieved. For almost a year he was close to catatonic. Other survivors had to take care of Rick.

"It's weird that."

"What's weird Mr Archer?"

"That my first clear memories are from these random people that took care of me while my father went crazy. Don't even know their names, or where they are now. Just thought that was weird."

"Well, it is unfortunate that you lost your mother, and technically your father, at the time where cognitive functions began. Your development could only be impaired." Rick maintained his scowl for a few moments before getting back to his story.

Frank eventually snapped out of it, he found himself living in a crash site turned refugee camp. He would act. As far as he was concerned the ruling elite was responsible, they were the ones who profited from this war. The world governments had to be toppled, all of them. Unreasonable fascist leaders were running the nations that had once fought fascism. But their extreme and unrepentant rhetoric drew the ire of more and more people, including their own people. Frank would exploit these cracks.

During Frank's nap, the war had engulfed much of the world. Rick remembered his father being hysterical when he found out nukes were dropped. Vast swathes of desert were turned to glass, cities to dust and the people to ashes. Many more were bathed in radiation as fallout reached far and wide. Rioting ensued pretty much everywhere a bomb wasn't dropped. The massive destruction in the Middle East, Asia, U.S and much of Eastern and Northern Europe had put a damper on things. People didn't want to fight anymore. The average Joes were reaching a breaking point; they had finally had enough of dodging explosions on their way to Starbucks. Rick stopped, something had darkened in the doctor's features. Was he one of those average Joes? *Not a good time to be alive, war.*

Frank spent days and nights feverishly writing about the state of the world. It consumed him. If he could reach enough people maybe he could help stem the madness. Things appeared to be at a stalemate. Countries just traded ordnance while people starved and lived in fear. Around the time Frank woke up, about a year into the war, hackers blew the lid wide open on the dirtiest of secrets. It was one of those cases where Frank would have rather been wrong. A treasure trove of leaked documents confirmed some of his worst conspiracy theories. It was all a corporate grab for planet Earth, orchestrated with financial institutions and puppet governments. The elite's goal was to suppress the populations' awakening by keeping them busy with war. Also on the agenda, decimating the younger generations and re-distributing remaining resources through the elimination of smaller nations. Just thinking about that world, those people, made Rick seethe with rage.

It had taken a little while for the proper amount of outrage to build up. Mainstream media had tried to suppress the information but it was too late, there was no stopping it now. "The cat's outta the bag". Frank's aptly named article had gone viral. In it, he exacerbated people's feeling of betrayal. All were puppets and had been for generations. All lived and died on the whims of an insane elite. Wars were orchestrated for social restructuring. Human advancement or lack thereof was meticulously planned and controlled. Happiness was precisely administered in small enough dosage that people wouldn't emancipate from mental slavery, but not so much that they wouldn't fight. Fear and hate were carefully cultivated so that people consumed and remained divided, paralysed to do anything else. "And as we consumed our planet we turned it into shit."

"I never expected such poetics from you..."

"These are not my words. They're my father's words. Where'd you think I got my potty mouth from?" Rick was pleased the doc smiled. "You know swearing is a great way to express emotions. Like spoken emoji." He laughed, "you should try it sometime." Rick laughed some more, he was feeling more relaxed. "OK, where was I? Oh yeah, my dad was furious. Like, a level of wrath he'd never felt before. He wanted to commit unspeakable acts of violence on those responsible. He wanted to squeeze the life out of them, watch it escape through their bulging eyes. His words." The doc winced at the image. Rick could still remember his father making the gesture while pacing angrily.

THE FUTURISTS

Frank knew it was time to leave his island paradise turned refugee camp, and head back to the grim reality of battle-torn Europe. Rick was going home. Frank had heard civilian groups were organising, the smell of revolution was in the air, and he wanted to be a part of it. He'd booked passage on a ferry to northern Spain, and a few days later they were back on European soil. Those few days, on the boat to Spain, were Rick's first pleasant memories. He and his father sitting on the deck taking in the Ocean's majesty and the fresh air. The lasting memory of the crisp wind stung Rick. It'd been a long time since he'd breathed that kind of air. Rick had later found out that during those quiet times, Frank had been deep in thought, planning.

Frank was a techie, and his revolution started online, finding and organising the disgruntled and disillusioned. That's when he'd gotten the idea for the Futurist Party. A way to beat governments at their own game. A cross-border political party to wrest control from the establishment. A movement focused on science, technology and unity. For the logo, Frank had decided on a group of silhouette people forming an upward arrow to the future. And for the motto, he'd chosen: "We are not right! We are not left! We are forward! We are Futurist!" It quickly became a song, Rick remembered trying to figure out how to sing it with his father. They ended up splitting it, chanting the first bit and singing the second bit.

"Interesting…"

"What?"

"Hmmm? I was just thinking this was interesting, I'd never really thought about the Futurist chant and how it came to be."

"Great, are you done? Can I go back to my story?"

"Yes sorry, I'll try to keep my mumblings to myself." Rick was starting to think maybe this guy was alright.

Frank believed if they could get the Futurist Party elected worldwide the lines between countries would blur, and there would be unity. The trillions of dollars spent on weapons every year would be free to be invested in improving the world. It was a utopian dream, but the suffering and despair of the last years had made this kind of ideal achievable. *People were pissed off.* The time for the pursuit of a technological and environmentally conscious society had come, and Rick was sat in the room when the Futurist manifesto was crafted. The original hand scribbled document that would shape the new world had some of his spit on it. This detail always made the crowd laugh, the doc did smile. *Good enough.*

Frank's reasoning was sound enough to seduce the masses. Finished with the greedy ways of the past. Equilibrium, not growth. His articles went out daily, haranguing the masses. *Wake the fuck up!* His following had grown into the millions, and he spent his days on social media, writing and sharing. Spreading the word. These were not fun times for Rick.

Frank believed the change had been waiting to happen for years, constantly impeded by the remnants of the industrial age. He preached a complete re-evaluation of how humans produced and managed food. His articles inspired people to believe a new world could be built, from the ground up, using smart technologies to transform the planet. He wrote of the post-capitalist economic models needed to support this new not-for-profit society. Obviously, this was all way too complicated for Frank or any one man. No, the idea was to get the ball rolling, publish the start of a manifesto and call for thinkers, artists, any and all progressive minds to join the movement and help shape it. Whatever the Futurists amounted to it couldn't be worse than the perpetual cycle of war. If they failed, apocalyptic wastelands would cover the world as doomed models of growth-economy and greedy men continued to rape the planet. Rick sniggered and asked the doc if he remembered the political cartoon his father had circulated.

"You must remember it. Sexy planet Earth, with a butt, crack and all, and a bunch of fat cats in top hats fucking it, with ocean tears? And, in blood dripping red, the words: "YOU are letting THEM rape your MOTHER!" Powerful stuff. You sure you don't remember?" Rick eyed the doc carefully. "Of course you remember." He laughed, called the doc a pussy, and got back to spinning his tale.

The concepts of the Futurist Party spread like wildfire and were accompanied by massive military and civil disobedience. Groups popped up everywhere with one common goal. Take down the ruling elite. So began the end of the old world, the world of man. Frank was surprised by how quickly everything happened. He'd just seen embers and fanned them. Now the fire was out of control.

The establishment was also surprised. Mostly by the level of organisation demonstrated by civilian groups. The hacker collective known as Anonymous pledged its support to the Futurist movement and all those who would fight to free themselves. They'd gotten in touch with Frank one night, and suddenly he had power. Together, they targeted the banks, companies, individuals and governments that profited from war. In the space of a few months, they'd taken all the belligerents money and had destroyed or crippled their organisations. The identities of those labelled enemy of the people were leaked, and throughout the world, mob justice reigned supreme. Without money the elite no longer had control. For years the political and ruling classes were hunted down mercilessly. Those who profited from the misery of their fellow humans were driven to extinction. After which the people turned on themselves, settling old scores, mostly religious crap.

Frank was not in a great place during what is now referred to as the Great Purge. He had achieved more success than he could have ever imagined. He had started a movement that toppled the old world but had failed to realise how many people would burn and hang while words he had written were chanted. It messed with his mind. It messed with everyone's mind. Rick and the doc made eye contact, the purge was fun for no one.

When the dust finally settled, five years had passed. Rick was nine, and his life had been spent in hiding with an obsessive man who alternated between uncontrollable joy and soul-crushing sadness. Rick still didn't have any friends. Frank had been a hermit since he started the Futurist movement. The moment that site went online there had been a target painted on his back, and Rick's, *which is great when you're a kid...*

But there was hope now, the year was 2025, and there were no nations to speak of, organised religion was no more, iconic buildings symbolic of the corrupt patriarchal oligarchy were gone. Nothing but charred remains where the castles of old once stood. The war had wiped out the last remnant of the industrial age, the people and companies of that time were gone, gas and coal would never burn again. Unfortunately, the establishment had not gone quietly into the night. The world was scarred by conflict. In many places the air was unbreathable and the water undrinkable. The time to build a better world had finally come.

Frank's Futurist manifesto had grown far beyond his control, yet he was revered as a hero of the revolution. His face and the Futurist logo were spray-painted in cities all over the world. *And the fucking statues.*

"Don't you like the statues?"

"Yeah, they're great." *Dick.*

"I see they exacerbate your inferiority complex."

"I don't have an… You know what? Fuck you. I don't have to defend myself." Rick turned away from the doc. He'd been sat down the whole time, on edge, now he decided to lay back and look out the window. "During this whole unpleasant purge business, we'd been living in the Alps between France and Switzerland, near CERN." In Frank's thinking if a dark age came about this was where the phoenix would rise from.

From his hideout, Frank had created the Futurist website, managed memberships, moderated the forums, kept the news up-to-date and updated the manifesto with contributions. That was the extent of his revolution. He hadn't strangled a single greedy, corrupt bastard himself. He'd never had a plan beyond getting the ball rolling, and now the revolution was done. It was time to rebuild. The world would descend into chaos if something didn't happen soon. Since the banking system had gone down, people had gone back to bartering systems, in the civilised places. Other places had a law of the jungle vibe going on. Ironically, Anonymous, who had embraced the Futurist movement and spread it to the far corners of the world, had to become the system they'd helped destroy.

Frank realised leaving the old system behind was altogether too brutal, it needed to be phased out gradually. During the last few years of the purge, when people started turning on each other, he'd realised that anarchy would destroy the Futurist ideas. Anonymous had to set up a universal cryptocurrency banking system. They supplied everyone with an eWallet and a ton of spending money. The gazillions of dollars confiscated from the warmongers made every remaining human on the planet wealthy. Anonymous also set up universal basic income and a tax system, as well as the usual social services systems. Once they got the ball rolling others joined the effort in building a better world. Many on the Futurists forums called for Frank to lead, he was being hailed as the father of the revolution. But he'd never thought of himself as a leader, so he ignored the calls. That made him hate himself. "I mean everybody is out there... Rebuilding and shaping the new world. And we just sat at home. Watching the news. Hiding. Because he felt inadequate. I remember the frustration. The yearning for something to happen. I still remember the first time he saw them calling for him on the news. He shut down for a while after that."

"A lot of responsibility was thrust upon him. Most men would buckle under such pressure. But he rose to the challenge."

"Eventually... But that's the point. People only remember the great events of his life, they ignore the darkness and loneliness in between."

"You can't expect people to know the inner-workings of your personal relationship with your father, and you can definitely not be mad at them for not knowing. What matters is that he came through in the end."

"It was all a fluke."

"Not everybody uses luck to change the world. To first have luck, and then use it effectively is a rare thing. Some would say you're lucky!" Rick made a face that said "I don't agree" and got on with his story.

From the moment the Futurist got organised things changed rapidly and forever altered humanity. Without religious guilt and corporate greed humanity embraced technology and accelerated its merger with it. Frank had touched on the Terminator Syndrome in the manifesto; the fear of being destroyed by an AI that judged humans to be inferior. Frank posited that the only logical way to stop AIs and robots from taking over the world was to become like them. Humans transformed into cyborgs. With cybernetic implants, humanity started thinking on higher levels. The creation of time-dilated virtual learning drastically accelerated evolution. The smarter humans got, the easier it became to solve age-old problems.

Frank Archer brought about the pairing of humans and AIs, the merger of man and machine, the first mutants; he was the father of Transhumanity. The age Homo Cyberneticus had begun. Rick had sat back up and was eyeing the doc carefully. Usually, at this point in the story, someone joked that it was ironic that he was the last human. *Nothing.* Rick had had enough.

"Isn't my time up?"

"We have a few minutes left. Tell me about the circumstances in which you became the last human."

"Fine" Rick grunted. "My father was invited to join the

first Futurist Council, and for ten years there was peace and the expansion of a new civilisation. My dad was a father to this new humanity but to me, not so much. The war, the revolution and the rebuilding consumed my father's life and robbed me of my childhood."

"There was obviously a bigger picture that neither children nor teenagers are good at seeing. But Rick, you are a grown man now. Surely, now you understand."

"Meh, in any case, I didn't then, so I rebelled and left Zero City 1 to travel the world."

Those years were good, Rick partied a lot, he smiled as he remembered those carefree days. He became the last non-modified human by pure chance. Some twenty years ago he was staying in a colony in New Zealand far from the burgeoning cyborg-mutant conflict. The cyber upgrade and genetic mutation crazes hadn't swept the region so much yet. Changes were still utilitarian or medical in those times. But the craze came. While Rick was travelling... *Shouldn't have stopped by Bangkok.*

Rick got word his father was dying and left New Zealand to make his way home to Zero City 1. When he eventually got back to France, he was flagged at a station. Rick had thought he was in trouble, but the security AI had merely picked up that he was free of all cybernetic implants. Relieved and slightly annoyed he'd headed to his father's home without thinking much more about the event. He had new problems.

Frank Archer was gone. There had been a funeral, but there was no body to cremate. No one knew where his father's body was. Rick had missed saying goodbye to his father. He'd missed the ceremony. "He left me here to rot..." Rick was still angry and a bit sad.

The silence offered the doc an opportunity to make an observation sure to please Rick. "I find it interesting that you've spent all this time talking about your father, trying to bring out his failings. Do you feel you have not achieved as much as him? Do you see him as a hero? While perhaps you see yourself as a failure?"

"He became a hero accidentally...He didn't do much..." Rick's voice trailed off, even he didn't believe his cynicism.

"Didn't he? I just heard the story, and it seems to me like he did plenty. More than you or I. Are you angry that he left you before you could show your worth?" The doc watched intently, but Rick showed no reactions. *Poker face.* "Let me tell you. You are not a failure! Your very existence maintains a fragile peace between the children of humanity." *Trying the saviour angle.* Rick thought that was desperate.

"The immortal cyborgs and their mutant children will always be at odds." Rick's voice was powerful and ominous for an instant, and then it deflated, tired and sad. "There is no need for me to continue being a show monkey. It serves no purpose, it's futile, and it's driving me insane. I want my life back."

"No, what you want is to get out of your contract, get cyber implants and go off into space." *Got to hand it to the doc, hit the nail on the head with that one.*

Rick's time was up. He got up, grabbed his mask and jacket, and left without another word.

AMY

Amy was floating by the door. She was Rick's assigned AI. A Smartcube. Most people had one. She'd been appointed to Rick when he was a teenager. Now, Smartcubes like her were assigned at birth. She'd followed Rick around everywhere since they'd been paired. Each AI was unique and had personality traits derived from its ward. Amy's body was a fifty-centimetre cube powered by solar rechargeable nanowire batteries, she also had a diamond battery backup system. In theory, she could last forever. Smartcubes had replaced smartphones, all personal devices really. She was a living-sentient-immortal quantum computer, but she'd spent the last thirty years babysitting an addict. That was her lot in life. To serve as guardian, mentor, bodyguard, advisor and friend to Rick Archer. He was crazy, but Amy loved him like a brother.

At first, AIs were like babies. But they learnt fast, a few days on the internet and they were all caught up. Over time they developed their personality in tandem with the person they were matched with. As a result, Amy had taken on many of Rick's traits…

One of the Smartcubes' more popular functions let people choose the voice and personality traits of a celebrity or anyone with video and sound records. Some people even used family members. Amy wasn't always Amy. She'd started life as SC-117. *Not great.* She liked Amy better. Rick had chosen some pre-war comedian as the basis. He found her hilarious. She'd taken on some of her personality traits as well as the voice.

The door to the office opened, and Rick stepped out.

"Let's go, Ames." She followed him out into the lobby.

Brock was waiting there. Brock Dynamite was a beast. Inferable from the name. It was also easy to tell by looking at him. He had dedicated his life to being a badass. Brock loved cyber implants and eighties action movies. Seeing him in all his glory made that clear. This nine-foot mountain of bulging muscle and shiny metal was unfuckwithable. Amy loved Brock. He was the only one who could manage bad Rick. Since his assignment to Rick life had been more manageable for her. As Rick's bodyguard, Brock had to stop him from hurting people and himself. No easy feat.

Amy only knew a little about Brock. He didn't talk much about his past, and his files were sealed. She'd tried to access them long ago. Eventually, he'd opened up to them, a bit. His childhood had not been fun. Brock was born during the war, and his parents had died early on, leaving him to fend for himself. He was feral during the purge. Brock had been saved by a deserter who'd been finding the war's orphans and taking care of them. Cyber implants had fixed his trauma and allowed him to control his rage. That's about as much as she knew about his youth.

Brock had a slight addiction to upgrades. Though Amy had to admit she was fond of his now iconic green-mohawked face-tatted warrior-god look. Terrifying to behold but cool.

Wherever Brock went, Mr T followed. Brock had modelled his appearance after the A-Team star and picked his voice and personality for his AI. It never got old having him float about shouting "I pity the fool!" Brock let Mr T do a lot of the talking for him. It intimidated people, and Amy found it hilarious.

Back on the streets of Zero City 6, night was coming, and the rain was still pouring. It was about time to drink if Amy knew Rick. The city was built on the ruins of London and the entire south-east of England. Like the others, it was a massive thing.

The Zero City concept was one of Frank Archer's great achievements. And one of his favourite stories to tell, Amy had heard it a hundred times. Frank had been exploring the futurist forums, he'd come across a thread about Zero City 1.

The perfect Futurist city, zero waste, zero emissions, egalitarian social system, automation and AI assistance, all that good stuff Frank was about. Thousands of people had collaborated on this virtual city project. Frank had taken the thread and made it front and centre of Futurist goals. "I'll see those cities built" he'd say, "and I did" and he'd laugh and people would cheer. She'd always found him charming. Never quite understood why Rick was so angry at him. *Human stuff.*

Zero City 6 had been easy to build. The entire area had been flattened by a Russian fleet during the war. Very little was left of old London, but the area had recovered in no time. Now, a hundred million people called the city home.

Amy was one of the wide variety of sentient "people" that defined transhumanity. Defunct humanity's closest relatives were the cyborgs; humans with cybernetic implants, nanobot colonies, biomechanical limbs and bionic organs. Though those who most looked like humans were the mutants. Genetically enhanced humans. Proportionally perfect, supersmart, super-strong, the Superman-Greek-god thing going on. Humanity's descendants also included the AIs like Amy who managed the world and its people. AIs were only outnumbered by the Androids and Robots. All had representatives on the Council that governed Transhumans. Apart from Rick. No representatives for the human.

Rick looked at Brock, Mr T and then Amy. "We're going drinking." No surprise there.

Amy let out a girlie "woohoo!"

In their infinite wisdom, the architects of digital minds had introduced Artificial Stupidity. Amy could understand the little things like sin and fun. It turned out, alcohol, drugs, sex and all that emotional stuff was crucial in getting machines to be more human and help them attain true consciousness. For this reason, it was possible for artificial minds to get fucked and fuck and enjoy it all.

"Where to?"

Brock had some upgrades that meant getting him drunk was near impossible, or just very expensive, so he rarely enjoyed it. It was also when he had to work the hardest. Over the years Amy and Brock had tried to shame Rick into showing more restraint by getting Mr T to record his antics and putting them online. But it had only made Rick more popular.

"I pity the fool that doesn't go to the Purple Flamingo!" Mr T had spoken.

"The usual then" Rick started walking, showing little concern for the rain.

The Purple Flamingo was a roof bar in one of the many underground pit chambers. The pits had served as the ultimate steam blow-off since their inception. Amy had to admit the solution was elegant. Humans were animals. Intelligent but victims of their emotions and instincts and their descendants were more similar than they liked to admit. Zero Cities had been built with their ancestors' weaknesses in mind. AIs knew this but were mature enough not to rub in the face of their wards.

Amy thought the designs were great. The original plans had imagined the cities as seven concentric circles. An outer ring of forest, nature and play. A much needed close-by getaway for those seeking to escape the urban cityscape. The nature ring seamlessly merged with the farmland ring; which was also home to retirement zones and early education centres. The young learnt from the old about their world and nature and how to live in harmony with it. The green outer rings were separated from the urban rings by a water-filled ring, it served no real purpose but making the fourth and sixth rings pleasant. Rick lived in one those prime locations with a beautiful view of the ring lake. Amy had tried to take him there countless times. Not once had they gone. She understood though. Rick was surrounded by happy families living in lush residential areas dotted with parks and high school teenagers up to no good. Rick didn't belong. The house had been assigned to him based on merit and under the assumption that he would start a family. Instead, he spent his time past Robot Town and the giant skyscrapers deep in the pits. Rick's favourite place of all could be found in the centre of every Zero City. The pits.

Dug as deep as the city's foundations the pits spread beneath like an ant colony. These holes were filled with wicked fun. It was always night time in the pits and people could catch a drink, a fight and a whore in the same place or weirder stuff... Apparently, the pits were similar to the old world's night markets and red light districts, places like Vegas and Amsterdam used to be. Rick loved the pits. He'd dragged Amy to every pit in Zero City 6. As well as many a pit the world over. *Rick really loves the pits.*

Zero Cities were designed for ten million inhabitants give or take a few. Not a hundred million. Zero City 6 was actually eleven Zero Cities built next to each other. London was slightly larger and in the centre, the others spread around it like petals on a child's terrible rendering of a daisy. All cities had grown clones over time, though shapes changed from city to city.

Zero City 1 started in Paris and covered all of Northern France up through Belgium to Holland and bits of Germany. It's where Rick had grown up and where Amy was born.

Zero City 2 started in Berlin and encompassed Hamburg and Prague, it was Rick's favourite for pits. Zero City 9 covered most the US East Coast. Rick did not like it there.

The list went on, with major Zero Cities in all parts of the world. Some inhabitants had chosen to live outside of Zero Cities. Amy had only ever travelled with Rick, and he'd never shown any interest in travelling for the sake of travelling. There's so much she wanted to see. Lately, she'd been obsessed with the Aquacyborgs living in harmony with the ocean dwellers. She'd seen them once, but they'd learnt to communicate with sea mammals since. *They talk to dolphins.* The idea fascinated Amy, and she knew a part of Rick cared, a part she hadn't

T.F.R. LeBoomington

seen in a long time.

THE PIT

It was a few dozen blocks to the nearest pit, Rick had done a block before he decided against walking the whole way. He was drenched and couldn't see anything out of his steamed-up mask. He had two options, grab the train or a car if he could find one. Cars, or what was referred to as cars, were glorified golf carts with bumpers, great fun to drive. *When it's dry. Train it is.* Rick headed to the nearest metro entrance and hopped on the inner maglev train. All inner trains went to the pit, and all outer trains went to the green zones. Circle trains went around in circles. It was a good system. Rick liked it. It was about twelve minutes to the pit stop. Enough time for a pre-drinking nap. Rick was forty, but the constant abuse to his body and the lack of upgrades made him feel a lot older, and look it, and people reminded him of that, often. *Fuckers.*

"Wake up!" Brock delivered what he must have thought was a soft punch, expertly to Rick's arm.

"What the fuck!" Rick jolted awake eyes darting left and right. "Fuck that hurt. Fuck you."

"We're here, let's go!" Brock got up and pulled Rick who made a show of his dead arm by flapping about like a seal.

There was a steady stream of people hurrying into the darkness. Most people stopped by the cloakrooms to leave valuables. There were cloakrooms at every pit entrance. It was sweltering in the pit, and people didn't take anything they weren't prepared to lose. The queue was long but time flew by. Rick spent it watching people stumbling out into the light. They covered their eyes and screeched like vampires in sunlight. They avoided eye contact at all costs for fear someone might see the shame in their eyes. Rick didn't have any shame. That was his superpower, he didn't feel embarrassment or humiliation like others. His field of fucks to-give was barren.

Sometimes a group would stumble out of the pit. That was rare. People always lost their minds and their friends in the pit. *At least I do.* Rick was not impressed by those guys. It just meant they had upgrades like Brock's, more resistance. He'd like to see them try to party like a human, with good ol' human organs. Rick's turn was up, and he left his gas mask and jacket, he also left his shirt, shoes and socks and emptied his pockets. *No need for any of that.* Amy bought the drinks anyway and the food, and did the taxes... She did everything really.

Once he was rid of his stuff, and Amy had saved the cloakroom number, they were off. Rick was salivating like a deprived alcoholic. He hurried into the familiar darkness, the echo of his feet slapping against the stone floor joined the vibrations of a thousand tunes being played by as many bars. The winding paths were dotted with alcoves where merchants peddled their twisted wares. They knew Rick's name, and they called out to him, but he had no time for them right now. He needed to drink, and think about things while drunk. Decisions had to be made. Not the kind of decisions sensible people made.

The Purple Flamingo was one of the crew's favourite watering holes. The place had a jungle thing going on, Rick loved the fake trees with treehouse table booths in the branches. The main attraction was an artificial pond where anibots frolicked. They had purple flamingos, obviously, but the cheeky monkeys were more fun to watch. They were programmed to mess with each other, other anibots and patrons. Rick liked watching stupid tourists lose their minds on the monkeys that were programmed to return their crap anyway.

The place had a chilled summer vibe, deep house beats were playing, and the illusion of being somewhere else was convincing. Projectors, screens and holograms created an idyllic scene of a lagoon and sandy beaches. Spotlights gave them the sunlight and warmth. It was hot in there, hotter than the pit, which was already sultry beyond tolerable. To counter the heat, little pipes with holes poked in them diffused refreshing water on patrons. Like the pit expert he was, Rick was practically nude. As a human, he didn't have the fancy body temperature regulators enjoyed by many cyborgs. He'd gotten the idea from mutants who mostly dressed like surfers. They loved to show off their flawless bodies. *Sexy bastards.* But they had the right idea, it made the pit more enjoyable.

The entrance to the bar was down a plant-lined pathway off one of the main tunnels. The place was packed, but Amy called ahead every day to ensure Rick's table would be ready. He didn't even have to ask, Amy knew. Most people had a neural link with their AI, not Rick though. He didn't have the neural interface upgrade. Still, Amy knew him like they had a link. Or maybe Rick had become too predictable.

Rick's table overlooked the artificial pond and anibots, as well as the entrance, bar and many of the other tables. It was an excellent place for people watching. The Purple Flamingo catered to everyone. Cyborgs, mutants, AIs, robots, androids and even humans. Which Rick knew really meant low-level cyborgs and mutants, all could get off in their own unique way. Amy had ordered a round for the table.

Drinks mostly came in edible bubbles. Better for the environment, *and cool as fuck.* Some drinks were still served in glasses and bottles made of the same materials, just thicker. Amy got herself an electric blue bubble of something with actual electricity coursing through it. She hovered above her bubble, and a telescopic straw came down. The drink was mixed with what robots, androids and AIs referred to as dumb juice. Amy loved the feeling, she often reminded Rick of that during their sessions. From what he understood the drinks were laced with magnetic disruptor particles that simulated low battery or something. She'd said it jumbled her thoughts and made everything funny. Basically, it made them stupid drunk. Mr T got a Mellow Yellow Bubble. Rick never touched those on a night out, that was chilling at home booze. Brock drank some Japanese firewater that could start a twentieth-century tractor. It was called Purple Brain Bubble Blaster, PB3, it had a crazy Japanese name like Papuru Baburu or something. If Rick had any of that, he would drop dead. He really wanted some. For years he'd wondered what it tasted like. In response, Brock had always ordered the strongest thing a human could handle and made Rick drink that. And every time it broke Rick, drove him completely insane and for days they'd lose him in the pit.

"So…" Rick started. He poked a hole in his bubble with his tongue and sipped a bit of his rum before downing it. He made that face you make when you've just had your first shot. He chewed on the bubble for a bit and started again, "have you guys ever been to the Moon?" He turned to the waiterbot, "Keep 'em bubbles coming."

"I have not, but I have files on it. The Moon is an astronomical body that orbits Terra, it is Terra's only permanent natural satellite. The average distance of the Moon from Terra is 384,400 km or 1.28 light-seconds…"

Mr T turned to Amy "Shut up, fool! Stop your Jibba-Jabba!"

Brock was not amused. Rick thought it was funny though.

Amy faced Mr T and continued "The Moon is in synchronous rotation with Terra, always showing the same face…" Amy started orbiting Mr T without breaking eye contact. Rick chuckled.

"Shut up, all of you". An exasperated Brock turned back to Rick. "Why? Do you want to go to the Moon?"

"Maybe, I don't know… I was just making conversation" Rick looked away, scanned the bar for some action, then looked back at Brock. "So have you been to the Moon?"

"Long ago, for a mission. Not much going on there. Just factories and research. Boring. Only one pit, so don't know what you'd do there."

"What about Moonland and Luna City and the Low-G theme park and the fucking alien artefacts?" Rick was annoyed now. "How could you not be curious. How could you not want to see the first city humans built outside of Earth? Or the fucking alien moon base!?"

"It doesn't sound all that great. Seen the alien stuff on TV." Rick thought Brock was an ignorant pain in the ass at that moment.

"Well do you like museums?"

"I don't see the..." Rick cut him off.

"Just answer the question. Do you like museums?"

"No, not really I guess. I haven't really thought about it. You wanna see something you look it up. Crowds, children everywhere. Sorry. Museums don't do it for me."

"Fuck you! Don't apologise to me. Museums are great, you're just too smart to know you're stupid." Rick continued, he had to press his advantage. "You don't appreciate things enough. You think like a machine. What about fucking emotions man? Don't you feel something when you think about humanity's journey to the stars? The Moon is where it started man. Fuck." Rick reached forward and grabbed a rum bubble.

"But it's a boring shit hole, and nothing is going on there." Brock reached for one of the brutal purple bubbles.

"Ok, fine. How about Mars?"

"What about Mars?" Rick could tell Brock was getting irate. More irate than usual. Brock was always angry when he was drinking.

"Have you been to Mars?" He enunciated to make sure Brock understood.

"I have not. But I looked it up, and Mars is the fourth planet from the Sun and the second-smallest planet..." Amy was on her second bubble, she was getting funnier.

"Shut up Amy! Crazy fool!" Mr T played his part too.

"Both of you shut the fuck up!" Brock waited for the laughter to die down. "No, I haven't been to Mars. I did think about travelling Solus long ago... But then I got the job babysitting you."

"Don't you still want to? I mean it's the first planet we colonised and terraformed. It's a pretty big thing. No?" Rick switched to his most serious face. "Brock, mate, I'm dying, and I have a bucket list. I want to check the items off this list before I die. I need you to help me." No response. "I want to see the Moon, I want to go to Mars, and I just want to go into fucking space before I die."

"Rick that's not funny! And you know I can't let you break your contract. You don't want to fuck with the Agency or the Council for that matter."

"I thought you were my friend. And I'm not joking. I am dying. Maybe not right now, but I will at some point. This contract is murder. They are killing me, and you are letting them." *OK, that was a bit dark.*

Brock seemed a little hurt by that last one. "I am your friend, but that's beside the point. It's my job to keep you safe and get you to your gigs. You turn on the Agency and Council and no one will be able to keep you safe."

"So you work for the Agency then, and the Council, you serve their interest. My life is meaningless to you beyond a paycheck. You're just a tool like that psychiatrist and Barry that fucking jewbot cunt. All tools used to keep me in check."

"Listen, both Barry and I have your best interest at heart."

"Fuck you, it's my best interest within the parameters of your best interest. I want to be free, I want to be me, I want to change. Everybody in this world can, but not me. That's not right!" Rick slammed his fists on the table "My body is my own... I should be able to do what I want with it."

"That's not for me to decide. I'm not the one who got into this insane contract and got to live the high life for ten years and now wants out. And I thought we had a good thing going..." *Trying a bit of reverse psychology.*

"Shut up you big fat pussy. My emancipation and our

friendship could work great together. You could be my bodyguard lover while we travel through space with our enemies hot on our tails."

"Fuck you, funny man. And anyway you wouldn't be able to afford me without the Agency lining your pockets."

"I have some money saved…" Rick lacked confidence. He knew his voice had betrayed him.

"Amy? How much does Rick have saved?"

"Amy don't you answer that shit! It's confidential! Fuck you, Brock!" Rick got up, grabbed another rum bubble and sucked it up. "Fuck you I'm leaving." He threw the crumpled up bubble on the table and stormed off. "Amy come on! Let's go whoring."

Rick expertly fell-slid his way down the stairs, then stumbled across the bar, knocking down tables and trays and bouncing off a few dancing couples. The second bounce sent him into the pond where the flamingos and monkeys played. Rick tried to get away from them. Laughter began spreading from table to table. Rick glared in Brock's direction. A couple of girls had already joined him. Brock attracted the ladies like shit attracts flies. They couldn't stay away from him. He was quite famous, being the Last Human's bodyguard for a decade was a pretty big deal. And he'd been Rick's bodyguard in movies and TV shows. He mostly used his fame the same way as Rick. For preferential treatment and getting laid.

FUCK'N'FIGHT

Rick found himself buzzed and propped up against a wall. It was dark and hot, and it sounded like everything was far away. He needed to get laid, his hormones were going crazy. He was horny. Really horny. He'd told Amy thirty times in ten minutes. Hopefully, she'd take him where he needed to be. Amy was a great wingman, she fired up her tractor beam and captured Rick's head. He loved that. However poor his attempts at walking were, he couldn't fall. This way she could keep him straight and lead him to his destination. It was a common sight in the pits. AIs leading their drunken humanoids from place to place, like drunk dogs on a leash. This only became a problem if the AIs were also wasted, but they had safeguards.

Amy knew how to handle Rick, she had his back, always. They even had sex once. Amy wanted to know what it was like with a human and Rick is down for anything at least once. They'd rented a blank android body and Amy had transferred to it. Then they'd done the deed. Rick had found it great, and Amy seemed to have enjoyed it. She'd told him it was great and they joked about it often. Rick knew it couldn't have been that great. He was only human. Amy had a small collection of bodies at home. She just used them for sex and often commented on the epicness of the act with cyborg and mutant super-gods. Rick had never understood why she only used the bodies for sex. She said she just preferred her cubic body.

Rick felt depressed suddenly. The reasons were so many,

The Last Human?

he was the world's village idiot after all, but right now it was that no one had ever described sex with him as epic. It was becoming unbearable to be ignored, chastised or laughed at every time he tried to bring anything up. Thankfully, Amy helped him get smashed and laid. It helped with the pain and loneliness, but this would no longer do. Something was burning inside of him. Rick was done being a good puppet, he was done playing. *Starting tomorrow*. Tonight Rick was going to play some more, he needed it.

People mostly just had sex for fun now. Rick found that agreeable. Without religion, people had moved beyond their ancestral shame. Reproduction had been redefined as the merging of two or more people. Couples, or groups even, designed their offspring which were grown in artificial wombs or assembled.... They came out perfect every time, and no more nine months of inconvenient sobriety. Seemed like a win-win to Rick. Few could afford it, but flying superhuman demigod children were an option. If Rick ever convinced someone to merge programming with him, he'd be getting one of those superman kids.

Sex was for fun, and nobody had crazier sex than the cyborgs. Well, maybe the post-birth mutants. Rick saw these guys lurking in the pits. People who chose to be modified after birth to look different or weird, usually weird. Transhumans had taken on every shape and form they could imagine. Often inspired by Manga. These days' people could just walk into a morph clinic and go "I'll have a couple of tentacles, some wings and maybe some dicks here and there, thanks." It all fascinated Rick. It didn't arouse him. He just found it interesting. From a scientific point of view.

Cyborgs knew how to party too. Rick had seen guys with rotating dildo wheels for genitals. People were installing mad contraptions in place of their parts, and the use of artificial skin and sensors meant they could feel it just like a human would, or more if they cranked the sensitivity up. So it was great, but instead of humans, people were turning into cocktacle dildo monsters for the night... *Good times.* Rick liked to watch, but he'd never considered partaking in live-action tentacle Hentai. It was a bit much even for him.

Gender was beyond fluid now, beyond gaseous; it was ethereal. People could wake up and go to sleep having switched genders a few times. Rick wanted to try it someday.

Amy picked Rick's favourite for the night's entertainment. She said he needed to get hard in every sense of the word, and this was the right place to do it. Maybe banging a girl while watching two demigods kick the crap out of each other would trigger massive hair growth on his balls. Maybe even give him the strength to reclaim his life. If he remembered anything whenever he came out of his daze. Rick had sobered enough to realise where he was. "Fuck yeah! Fuck'N'Fight! Fuckin' love this place! Boom! Amy, I love you!" Rick was trotting to his room, Amy released the tractor beam and let him go.

The main event was about to start. The arena was massive, but people in the stands were still hit by stray fireballs, and they loved it, like getting soaked at Splash Mountain. The arena was overlooked by a large Ultraglass dome adorned with charred spots and blood spatters. The glass screened hundreds of rooms with couches, beds, chairs, fuck swings, dildo wheels and whatever delights, tortures or comforts patrons might be seeking out. The show was going to be grand, it always was.

"It's room 144." Rick rejoiced. He loved that room. It had an excellent view, and boring crotchless chairs most didn't find fun. As a result, it had seen less action, and shining a black light in there would be less traumatising than say, any other room.

The fight hadn't started yet, and Rick was hurrying to his room. They entered the booth and he ran to the chair like a giddy child. "Rick is in the house! Let's get this motherfuckin' show started!" A waiterbot entered the room with a rack of bubble cocktails. Rick inspected the choice. "Boom!"

Amy was projecting the courtesan selection onto the wall, Rick took a gander. He stopped Amy on a petite human-looking girl. "Make sure she's sentient! Fucking a soulless robot is like masturbating, I can do it at home", Rick laughed. Amy not. He told her she needed to relax knowing full well it would annoy her slightly more.

The fight was about to start. Rick grabbed a bubble and an edible straw, the cocktail bubbles were sweet. He smacked his lips with delight as he got comfortable. He peered down at the fighters, both were obviously cyborgs. Rick turned to Amy. "So what's the deal?"

"The guy with the white and gold kimono and golden hair spikes is called Goldku. He's from Zero City 11 in Japan. He's a mutant with cyber implants including super speed actuators and muscle accelerators. Twice the menace. And he can shoot fireballs out his right arm. A single punch from him would explode your skull and send fragments across the sea to France. Oh, and he can also fly and levitate."

"Awesome! What about the other the guy? With the cape?"

"He calls himself Uberman. He's from the Berlin zone in Zero City 3. Same deal. Super-mutant-cyborg that can fly and levitate and can shoot laser beams out of his eyes. He could kick your nuts right up through your mouth and out to Luna." Amy's digital display lit up with a great big smiley face. Rick knew, she too loved seeing demigods get it on. *Filthy little AI is probably horny too.*

"Oooh yeah, this is going to be a good one." It was hard to follow the fights, those guys moved fast. Rick loved it anyway, it reminded him of watching Anime as a kid, and Amy recorded the fights and then projected slow-mo bits for him while doing a sportscaster's voice.

The fighters bowed without breaking eye-contact, the moment they were up straight, it was on. Both opened up with ranged attacks, firing laser beams and fireballs while dodging away. They pushed off against the back walls dashing towards each other to exchange lightning-quick blows. Combos of kicks, knees, punches and elbows. Relentlessly they blocked and struck each other, occasionally finding an opening. The speed and precision were dizzying for Rick. He could see flashes of action every time the titans made contact. Beads of blood and sweat flew out in circular shockwaves. Then Uberman seized an opportunity and flew above Goldku to unleash beam after beam on his staggered opponent. Goldku dodged the first few but was forced to block when he ran out of arena. People cheered as skin sizzled and metal scorched. Uberman raised his arms, and the crowd cheered even louder. At that moment Goldku seized his chance, he fired a barrage of fireballs and dashed towards his opponent. Uberman barely had time to block the fireballs before the follow-up fury. The crowd went wild. For a few minutes, they floated in the centre of the arena exchanging flurries of blows, their guards breaking more and more often as evidenced by the increasingly frequent spurts of blood.

Rick's eyes were glued to the fight when he noticed the girl's reflection as she came in. She was beautiful, long flowing blonde hair and crazy tattoos telling some sort of story. She looked human, but flickering lights beneath her skin betrayed her cybernetic implants. That was probably her real skin though. And her real breasts and her real vagina. All very important to Rick. She gracefully made her way towards Rick and Amy, who were both too engrossed to pay her much attention. The girl picked up a yellow-green cocktail bubble and approached Rick.

"Good evening sir, I am Lula, at your service." Lula handed Rick the bubble and waited for him to take the drink. Rick was not acknowledging her, the two fighters were still in the middle of the arena exchanging some of the most brutal blows he'd ever seen. Amy was going on about the shock waves and slow-mo, and stuff Rick just had to see. "Sir, I am Lula, at your service." She was a bit louder and insistent this time around, and Rick turned.

"Amy, keep watching and recording that shit." Rick looked up and down at Lula and then sucked his bubble dry before grabbing the one Lula was holding. "Thank you, Lula."

"You're welcome, sir."

"You can call me Rick."

"You're welcome, Rick. Now, what can I do for you Rr-rick." She rolled the Rs on the second Rick and leaned in closer gently rubbing her breasts against him. Amy let out a gasp, and he turned back to the fight. The fighters were on the ground facing off about twenty feet from each other, panting heavily.

Rick turned back to Lula and stood. "Yeah just get to work on my dick and balls", he expertly dropped his pants and sat back down into the chair. "Amy show me some of those super slow-mo shock wave replays." Lula did not like that.

"Excuse me SIR, but if you're going to be rude, I might as well just send a hooker bot." Lula was backing up, and if the next sentence wasn't perfect she'd be out the door, and it'd be synthetic pussy for Rick.

"Wait! I'm sorry, you're right. Let me try this again." Rick stood, his package hanging loose. "Kind lady of the night I am currently enjoying the climax of this fight between titans and was wondering if you could find it in your heart to pleasure my sensitive areas so that I too may climax. After which I promise to be more giving in our exchange and my little floating companion will surely find a way to reward such cooperation on your part." Rick offered a half-assed bow and his finest smile.

"That's better." Lula seemed amused; also she had to know who he was. Banging a celebrity was always good for someone's rep.

Rick watched some slow-mo replays with professional commentary courtesy of Amy, and he got an expert blowjob courtesy of Lula. The fight started again. There were no rounds, but fighters were quite civilised. They took little breaks when one or both were tired. And then started punching each other in the face again when they were both good and ready. This was such a time.

Goldku and Uberman gave each other the slightest of nods and got back to it. Fireball here, laser beam there, punch in the face, spin kick to the side of the head, now he's behind, kidney punches, grab the arm and flip him, then knee in the sides.

Basically an epic fight, both fighters going toe-to-toe the whole way. But guards were down, hits were getting sloppy. Someone else was struggling to keep it together. Tingles in his body, legs going straight, toes extending. Then both fighters went at each other full speed, flying-punch-to-the-face move. Double knock-out. The crowd went mental.

Rick exploded of joy in more ways than one. *What a sick fight. Pretty good blow job too.* Rick sniggered to himself. He was happy again, granted it didn't take much and it was fleeting. But he was happy in this moment, and that was the only way to be happy. *Which is weird, could someone be happy everyday but overall have a miserable life?* Rick didn't care, he wanted to ride the high. He banished his dark thoughts and focused on his company. He said some charming stuff to Lula who was paid to pretend it was the most charming shit she'd ever heard. Then they had sex. Once. It lasted a while longer than it usually did, Rick was on good form. He loved it and thought it was great, Lula was paid to tell him it was great. Once the deed was done Lula hung around for a bit, they had some drinks and watched some other fights. There was a clown fight going on when their attention turned back to the arena. Funny, but savage. Painting a giant hammer with bright colours and flowers didn't make it less brutal.

"So what's it like being the Last Human?" Lula had asked the question everyone asked, whether they meet him in person or he's giving an interview. Always that same question. *I don't know! What's it like not being human?*

"I guess being alive is being alive, so it probably feels the same for everyone. But if you're asking what it feels like being a human in a world of superhumans. Well, I can tell you that sucks massive hairy cheese balls."

"But what about being the most famous person on Terra?"

"I'm famous but not for the right reasons. I'm kept as a comedy sideshow, a reminder of why mutants and cyborgs should be happy." Rick got up and held up imaginary puppets. "Here look at the monkey dance, look how he is inferior, look how technology has made us better, all united against the human, now laugh at the monkey, look at him, laugh, just…" Rick slumped into the chair.

"I'm sorry, I didn't mean to upset you."

"It's fine, it's not your fault."

"For what it's worth I think you're funny." Lula smiled at Rick, it seemed genuine.

"Thanks. I think I'm going to go now." What goes up must come down. "Thanks for the great evening." Lula bowed gracefully and exited the room as quietly as she had entered. Rick sighed and looked down at the two clowns beating the crap out of each other with their oversized hammers. He turned to Amy.

"I want to escape Amy. I want out of this life."

"I know. Let's do it."

"I'm afraid. And even if I get what I want… I don't know what I'd do with my freedom."

"We do what you said earlier. We go to the Moon and then Mars. We do your bucket list."

"I was just trying to get under Brock's skin with that."

"But it's true enough, isn't it? So let's make it real. Let's do your bucket list."

"The Agency will never let me out of my contract."

"Well let's get a meeting in with Barry tomorrow and see if we can't change the Agency's mind."

Rick and Amy left their room and made their way back into the narrow dark tunnels of the pit. Rick was feeling a little better, at least now Amy was on board, and she'd help him. Not being alone was nice. A group of youths approached down the narrow tunnel to the bar. *Mutants.* These guys were fresh, they were just getting started, and people coming into the pit are usually the polar opposite of people leaving the pit. The corridor was narrow, even in the darkness they would recognise Rick. He would have to be face to face with each of them as they squeezed by. Sure enough, they recognised him.

"Holy balls, it's the Last Human!"

"Guys, look it's the Last Human!" The trio of bare-chested mutants looked like they were straight out of a Swedish nineties softcore porno. Longish blond hair and chiselled features, they had the Norse gods' look. Probably tourists from Zero City 5 in Denmark.

"Fuck no way!"

"Hey man let's get a picture together."

"Go away, leave me alone." Rick was trying to get away, but they followed him now.

"That's a bit rude man, we just want a picture."

"So fucking rude bro."

"Behaving like an ape basically, no manners, just a primitive creature." They pointed and laughed at Rick, like bullies in a schoolyard.

"What d'you say fuckface, I'm fuckin' Rick Archer bitch, fuck you!" He'd didn't see the punch coming. He was too drunk, and it was way too fast anyway. *That's all folks!* Weird thing to think when you get knocked unconscious.

ANOTHER DAY IN PARADISE

Rick woke with a pounding headache, like most mornings. This was usually followed by some staring at the ceiling wondering what the fuck he was doing with his life, all the while trying to will the hangover away. Flashbacks of his time in the pit started coming back. He had a good time. At least some of it was good. *Lost my shit on Brock. The fight was great. The sex too. I got punched in the face. Not so great that.* He felt his face with his hand and winced. At least he was allowed to take pain pills. And they were pretty effective. *Come here little buggers.* His bedside table happened to have a glass of water and a capsule of Pain Away in a small cup. *Love you, Amy.* There were a few other tablets in there, some stuff for his liver, some for his brain and his usual supplements. Rick popped all twelve pills at once, drained the glass and lied back down to resume his brooding. His happy-go-lucky attitude toward life seemed to be heading nowhere. *Well, actually...* He seemed to be heading for an early grave. *Wouldn't that be great!* The first person to die in years and probably the last. Forever known as the Last Human. The last human, dead. *Finally, free.* Rick thought back on his conversation with Amy. She was on board with his plan. *Or was it her plan? Whatever, the plan.* In any case, things were afoot. Amy floated into the bedroom. Rick sat up in his bed, did his morning cough and managed a basic greeting.

"Morning."

"Good Morning Rick!" Amy was chirpy as usual. "How are we doing today?" As Amy floated about the room, the blinds opened, and the speakers turned on. The news was going on about some unease somewhere in a system far away. There was also talk of the Last Human going viral overnight with some new videos. One of him playing with some monkey bots in the pond, one of him getting knocked out by a mutant teenager and one of him being carried home like a sack of potatoes while shouting some obscenities.

"Wha...?" Rick started, coughed, cleared his throat, and then rubbed his temples for a bit. "What happened last night?" He had just heard it on the radio but hearing it from Amy would make it real.

"What after you got knocked out or last night in general?"

"After the knockout..." Rick glared at Amy.

"The three guys laughed at you. Their Smartcubes recorded you, and they posted the video online. Would you like to see it? It's quite popular." Amy waited for a second or two. "No? OK. Then I called Brock, and he came to get you and carried you home." Amy hovered over, just in front of Rick. Her display showed a laughing face. "Standard procedure."

"Great." Rick didn't mean it. "Where's Brock?"

"He had two girls with him the whole time. They left after you were tucked in. Probably to bang." Amy floated off. "Up, up, up, busy day today. You've got a meeting with Barry this morning, Brock will meet us there, and then the Agency this afternoon. You remember the plan, escaping to a better life and all that."

"Hmmm ok." Rick got out of bed and headed for the bathroom. Amy stopped and turned back to Rick.

"You had a decent workout in the pit, so I've talked to Mom, and we've agreed you only have to do a twenty-minute workout. Enjoy!" Amy hovered off to the kitchen.

The Last Human?

Rick's house was smart, too smart if you asked Rick, but he had no choice in the matter. Rick lived in a residential area like most, and his house had an AI like every other building. Management AI's essentially ran buildings as efficiently as possible and kept their occupants healthy and safe. It's the healthy part Rick objected to.

Every home came with a modular workout robot, and each house occupant had to do a daily workout. There was no avoiding it, the house would lock Rick in and send the gymbot to give chase. No escape until the exercise was done. Rick tried to fight it sometimes, the gymbot always won. Just by trying to escape for a couple of hours he got his workout done. Best to comply, escape attempts were futile. *Just do your exercise.* The House AI communicated with the personal AI and based on daily data they calculated the adequate amount of exercise, which they then told to the gymbot. Rick hated that. That's why he tried to walk places and use stairs, he convinced himself it might spite the AIs if he had less exercise to do. He knew it didn't. They didn't care, as long as the numbers added up and the workout got done.

Rick dragged his feet over to the workout machine. Basically a Transformer all-in-one gym. Rick called the gym robot Guy. But that's because he woke up drunk and misread the label the first time.

"'Ssup Guy. What fresh new tortures have you devised for me today." Rick grabbed the smoothie bubble next to Guy and started sucking it up.

"Rick! Good morning!" Like most robots Guy was a chirpy annoying fuck. *Why are machines so fucking happy all the time?* "I've got more of the usual for you. Drink up your power smoothie and let's get you sweating."

"Gimme a minute." Rick finished his bubble and started stretching, Guy had started the playlist. The mood was set.

The exercise routine varied from person to person. Rick's had been designed for him by his AIs. Each aspect of his life was taken into consideration when planning his diet and exercise regimen. All calculated to maintain peak mental and physical condition at all times. Everything was customised to the individual's needs, taking cyber enhancements in consideration as well as lifestyle. The AI's were compassionate though, so they allowed cheating. *Sometimes.* Although Rick and debauchery went together like peanut butter and chocolate, he was pretty trim and in good enough medical condition. Though he was still the weakest person on earth. A baby could snap his finger off.

Rick got his workout done and headed to the bathroom. It had a toilet. Not a common feature anymore. Since the invention of quantum rectums, people just pooped in a sun somewhere. Many had upgraded. No need for toilets or toilet paper anymore. No fancy butthole for Rick though, he still had to wipe. Luckily for Rick, the quantum butt was only installed on eighty percent or so of the cyborg population. So toilets and paper were still manufactured in small batches for the remaining assholes.

Mutants had also done away with toilets in a creative fashion. Rick had always been intrigued by their additional organ that enabled them to fart odourless dust. Their clothes had a special butt pocket to evacuate the dust. The thought made Rick giggle.

Rick's toilet, like most toilets still in existence, was based on the pre-war Japanese smart toilets. Your butt was pampered, warm water jets, hot air and all. The experience was quite enjoyable once you got over the initial surprise. Rick loved to poop on his toilets, but even he had to admit the quantum anus was genius. It was only a miniaturisation of the solution for trash disposal, but someone had thought of it first and implemented it. Which couldn't have been easy, Rick imagined how that conversation might have gone down.

"I have a great idea!"
"What is it?"
"I'd like to put trash portals in people's butts!"
"You what?!?"
"You heard me."

The Last Human?

"That's actually genius. Here's a bunch of money."

Rick jumped in the shower after his daily toilet musings. The shower was out of this world. Hundreds of small jets created a thick mist, and diminished gravity levitated the water. It felt like being fully immersed in water but still being able to breathe. On the advert, they described it as bathing in the misty tail of a rainbow. The shower had a function that activated lighting angled perfectly to make rainbows. Pointless, but cool, and still a really lovely feeling. The lightness of the water and body created a sensation that was probably closest to showering in space. Or not, it's not like Rick knew anyway, only what the adverts said. Rick stepped out the shower into the body blow-dry zone. Clean Rick looked at himself in the mirror. He slapped his dick from side to side for a bit, tensed his muscles, made some faces and then went back into his room to get dressed.

◆ ◆ ◆

In the kitchen, Gousto was preparing breakfast. Gousto was the kitchen. His arms came out of panels hidden all over, like having a dozen trained chefs working in sync. Like Guy, he was merely an extension of the house AI. Rick had named the house AI MOM. It stood for Massively Overbearing Machine, Mom hated it. But calling the AI Mom was the only thing that made the bossiness tolerable. Rick had named the kitchen after that French chef in the rat cartoon. Gousto could cook anything as long as it was approved by Mom.

Gousto was good, but the most significant addition to the kitchen was Mr Food. A machine that makes food. Rick told it what he wanted, and it made it. He loved that machine. The device could make raw ingredients that Gousto could cook, or it could just make ready meals. Edible plates and all. The machine eliminated waste and the need for agriculture. Nobody knew how it worked. People had tried to figure it out. The machine's creator's identity was also a mystery. The Mr Food Inc company was equally mysterious. Rick had watched a documentary on it. He didn't care much beyond that, as long as the machine made him food, he was happy.

The machine looked like a large oven-fridge-like-thing got it on with a 3D printer. Stem cell cartridges were inserted into the back and a specialised AI, Mr Food, assembled the cells into the required foods. At first, Rick was resistant to the idea of eating artificial food. Amy had explained it to him over and over again. The food wasn't fake, those cells were assembled into beef, they were beef. The machine made superfood loaded with nutrients. And it turned out animals were far more aware than humans thought possible, and as a result, fear and sadness always made it into supposed real meat. *Not tasty ingredients*.

Rick, like everyone else, had come to love Mr Food. Animals must have really loved Mr Food because there was no longer a need to hunt them, herd them and slaughter them for their juicy meat. People still did it occasionally though, for sport and conservation mostly. Animals were all over the place, plants reclaimed land quickly, and beasts followed. Scientists had also cloned some species and brought others back from extinction, for funsies. This made the occasional culling necessary. Though for the most part animals no longer had any need to fear people. They were comfortable venturing into urban areas, even the inner circles of Zero Cities. Rick had seen some weird stuff in the pits.

Rick loved watching nature's ballet in his garden. By spraying different pheromone cocktails, the garden bot was able to direct, and to some extent communicate with animals, even have them contribute and help with gardening. The garden bots could have ants rake the dead leaves, spiders hunt mosquitos, birds target specific fruits or insects. As an added bonus the ability to communicate with animals had elevated nature documentaries to new heights, much to the delight of children like Rick. Cyborgs were also able to get augmentations that enabled pheromone communication. Rick would have loved the ability to communicate with animals. His mind wandered as he imagined himself as some cross between Doctor Doolittle and Tarzan, overwhelming enemies with his animal companions.

In the greenhouse, the gardener bot grew seasonal vegetables, herbs and fruits to accompany the meals. Mr Food could make that stuff, but some study had found that gardens were good for mental health. So... Gardens in every house. It was also apparently necessary to keep up agriculture education in case things went awry and Mr Food stopped working. Rick didn't know how to farm. He was already an adult when the new educational system started. The TV had educated him. Poorly.

Rick could smell his favourite cooking. Crispy bacon and pancakes. He wasn't sure he deserved his kingly breakfast, Amy's doing for sure. Rick found her hovering above the table using her tractor beam to bring up a food cartridge.

Amy didn't need food, but just like sex and drinking, she had been designed so that if she wanted to eat, she could. A great variety of meal simulations were available to AIs. The food itself was software stored on a data key. When Amy ingested it via her booze hole, it went through her artificial digestive system, so through a tube, and was expelled like a bullet casing after the program was downloaded. That bit was unnecessary, but Rick and many others thought it looked cool. The empty cartridge could then be refilled with a new meal experience. Amy had explained to Rick that the program simulated the taste and flavours of different bites and the sensations of meal satisfaction. Each aspect of the meal was recreated, each mouthful of each course and the atmosphere, from a candlelit dinner to beach BBQ, all elements were simulated.

AI's loved eating as a result. Everyone ate, cyborgs ate all kinds of foods. The types of food ingested depended on their level of cyber upgrades and modifications. Most required food with functional nanoparticles to help regenerate cybernetic components and ensure continued compatibility between parts. Robots ate information like AIs, and it came in many forms so that they could partake in meals with their fleshy counterparts. Their food could be programmed to simulate any flavour, so the way the meal looked was less meaningful to robots. Rick had often wondered about eating food that was programmed to taste a specific way. Humans had to cook fresh ingredients to perfection to enjoy a great meal, presentation and mouthfeel, everything needed to be right to even come close to the pleasure derived from a pile of drives programmed to taste great. Though for cyborgs food tended to be prepared and presented to perfection as well as programmed. They got the whole shebang. *One day.* Mutants ate like bodybuilding-Olympic-athlete-beast-monsters. They ate a lot, their obscene metabolisms demanded it. And they liked to talk about it, a lot, and make videos. *Perfect, beautiful douchebags.*

People just ate because they loved it. Getting together to eat was one of humanity's most enduring social constructs. Not this morning though, Amy was in her little world, and Rick wolfed down his breakfast with a sickening amount of maple syrup on his pancakes. He had Mr Food make some more twice before Mom put a stop to it.

"I'm going to make you work that off tomorrow." Mom's voice came out of nowhere and made Rick jump.

"Not if I burn it off today." Rick was in a defiant mood.

"That's a lot of sugar Rick, too much." Mom's voice had softened.

"I love maple syrup, like, really really love it." Rick picked up his plate and started licking it.

"Rick stop that."

"Sure thing." Rick put the clean plate on the table and looked up at one the cameras Mom used to see. "I have a big day today, needed the extra sugar." Rick left the kitchen and headed for the veranda. Amy didn't move, she was still enjoying her candlelit breakfast dinner. *Crazy AI.*

Rick plopped down in a deep leather chair overlooking the garden and grabbed a small wooden chest. He pulled out a crazy pipe shaped like a cross between a dragon and a silly straw. He set the box onto the side table and leaned back into the chair. After fumbling about in the box for a few seconds, he pulled out a handful of small pipette bottles. After examining the labels, he dropped a few back in the chest. With his left hand, he popped open the bowl receptacles at the front of his pipe. Balancing the pipe between his knees, he started to carefully drop liquid from the bottles in the different bowls on the pipe. Once done he closed the lids and dropped the bottles back in the chest. He leaned back and got nice and comfy before pressing a small button on the dragon pipe's underbelly. A small mechanism whirred to life, Rick started sucking on the dragon's mouth, and different coloured vapours rushed through the looping tubes. *Dragon Breath.*

Amy floated in. Rick barely acknowledged her. He laid back in his chair staring glassy-eyed into the garden. It was teeming with life, creatures small and smaller busying themselves with what seemed to be essential tasks. Rick was watching some birds have a conversation, wondering what they might be talking about. It looked like they were looking at him. Were they talking about him? Rick was so busy pondering the important things in life that he failed to react when Amy came to hover in front of his face.

"For fuck's sake Rick! Why d'you get high? You have important meetings today." *Shoo, little buzzkill.*

"It's fine Ames, chill." Amy's display flashed an angry red face.

"No, I will not chill! This is for you! But if you don't care and you're happy to carry on your self-destructive path we can just forget about everything! Let's just keep going like before!"

"Chill Amy, my first meeting is with Barry. I'll be fine by the time we go to the Agency. Though I might be drunk by then... It'll be after lunch!" Rick laughed, and Amy buzzed away angry.

"We're leaving in thirty. Stop getting high." Rick muttered "you're not the boss of me", took another toke of Dragon Breath and got back to staring into the garden.

The weather was good, the rain clouds had passed, and the sun was shining on a new day. Rick was lost in thought, relaxing thoughts, gazing lazily at the scattered clouds, the breeze gently shook the leaves, the bees danced about in the garden, and the birds sang a song about flying or something. Rick's thirty minutes flew by, and Amy came back into the veranda to ruin his peace.

"Time to go, I've ordered us a cab."

"Hmmm fine." Rick summoned all of his strength to beat gravity and rip himself out of the chair. "Where's Brock?"

"I've already told you! He's meeting us at Barry's." Rick seemed somewhat satisfied with that answer and mumbled a sort of acquiescence.

Gas mask, shoes, jacket and they were out the door. Rick said bye to Mom and followed Amy down the walkway. Their UberAIR was waiting on the street outside Rick's. The AI pilot greeted them as Rick took his seat in the front. There was nobody in the driver seat, so he liked to sit there. It reminded him of the good old days when humans could actually drive those things. In Zero Cities the only vehicles Rick could drive manually were the mini cars. Those little electric vehicles that were basically the offspring of bumper cars and golf carts. They weren't very fast, but quite fun. Everything else had to be operated by augmented people or AIs, for safety and whatnot.

SHOWBIZ

Rick remembered the first flying cabs as UberAIR took off quietly. The giant octocopter-car-planes made a lot of noise and were not as safe or stable as people would've liked flying vehicles to be. None of that was a problem since scientists had cracked anti-gravity. Something about exotic matter. Made no sense to Rick. Very few things made sense to him. He just observed the results. Making things fly and float had become far easier.

The cab headed for the centre rings of Zero City 6 - 3, near what used to be Brighton. Zero City 6 encompassed much of what was London, Surrey, Kent and Sussex. The rest of England had been reclaimed by nature after being bombed to smithereens during the war. There were smaller Zero Cities in Scotland and Wales and a few pre-war villages and towns that survived. The rest was either barren or reclaimed by nature. The bombings had been thorough, but that only meant it had been more straightforward to build something better on top. And Zero Cities were marvels of science, technology, architecture and social engineering. Much better than anything made before. Rick did regret the monuments. Too few of the old world's wonders were left. And though history taught that many of the great structures of the past were built by zealots and oppressors, they were still marvels to behold.

Rick had to admit that however great some monuments might have been their glory was diminished when the great

Zero Cities sprouted from the minds of humans. His thoughts returned to the scenery as the cab zoomed towards their destination and the giant towers came into view. *Like a spiked crown on a head.* Rick squinted at the lush lands of the mid-zone between Zero City 6-2 and 6-3. He tried to catch a glimpse of racers looping around on the acrobatic tracks. It'd always been a dream of his to race there, but it was reserved for augmented drivers. Just another way in which he got shafted.

It took about twenty minutes for Rick to get from his place in 6-1 to Barry's office in 6-3. Barry was set-up in a tower dedicated to entertainment. Thousands of levels filled with studios, sets and offices for those who worked in the entertainment industry.

Rick was fascinated by the mountain-sized conical towers that soared into the skies. They hadn't started off that tall, but as materials science advanced, and architecture evolved, the towers grew ever taller. The towers' shared bases spread beneath the entire city and deep underground, incorporating the Metro system and pits. Rick had little understanding of the science that went into building these behemoths, but he was suitably awed.

Towers were broken into sections and were filled with any activity the mind could conjure. People could get office space and do whatever the hell they wanted. Entire parks were built into the towers, some inside, some vertically on the outside and some open-air parks on platforms or in huge gaps. The building AIs, plants and smart materials all working together to make the towers pleasant, strong and stable. *How nice.*

The cab made its approach towards Tower 3, aiming for an empty landing pad a couple of levels above Barry's office. People were lounging in a park near the landing pads. The UberAIR's AI driver landed expertly, as always. *Here we go.* Rick put on his gas mask, jumped out the taxi and headed towards the stairs in the centre of the park. People immediately started to recognise him. Some smiled and waved from a respectable distance. Rick liked those people. Some ran at him screaming and demanding things. Things, like photos or videos or interviews for their blog. *Fuck you pay me.* He thought it but wished he could just say it. Though, he didn't fancy another punch to the face so abstained. Also, Brock wasn't here. *Where is that fucker?* Rick posed for a few photos, answered a few questions and said a few stupid things. He made a speedy exit before more bloodthirsty fans could find him.

Barry's office was in one of the waterfall atrium sections of the tower. One of the nicest office spaces Rick had ever seen. Not that he'd seen many others. The centrepiece was a massive waterfall spanning hundreds of levels in this section alone. Water collected from air moisture and rain by an advanced water collection system fed into the waterworks. Rick had once tried following the waterfall down from its starting point. It flowed inside and out, like a gravity-defying river, winding up and down through parks and office space and down the sides of the building. Stopping occasionally to feed a pond in a garden or a fountain in a plaza. It ran through glass tubes and down great waterfalls all the way to an outdoor pool hundreds of floors below.

A big plaque in the lobby explained that the architects had been inspired by the fabled Hanging Gardens of Babylon. Rick had to admit the result was a breathtaking feat of engineering and a beautiful expression of nature and art. Animals, robotic for the most part, frolicked in every green area giving the whole thing a lively atmosphere. As workplaces went, this was a good one.

Rick's office was in this tower. He didn't spend much time there. He only came in for meetings, shoots and to hang out at the Soho House pool bar. He was banned from there now. Pit behaviour was only accepted in the pit. His visits to the tower had somewhat diminished since the ban. He still had to come in at least once a week for The Last Human TV Show. *Nearing the end of season ten...* Just thinking about it made Rick cringe. He'd have to be there in a few days to shoot yet another humiliating episode highlighting his shortcomings. *Shoulda called the show*

Fail Much?

The studio was lower down in the tower. In a whole section dedicated to shooting movies and TV shows. Rick occasionally got offered movie parts. At best he was the comedy sidekick or victim but more often than not he was the idiot villain. Rick still took the roles because they were more fun than the TV show. *Any day of the week.*

The atrium was packed with people going to and fro. Working or pretending to work or not even pretending. People could get office space and just draw dicks on the walls all day, nobody would stop them, and some might also come in to watch and pay for the privilege. *It happened. Dicksy did it.* Rick had watched him work, they'd even had him on an episode. Turned out Rick wasn't very good a drawing dicks either.

Rick often wondered on what he'd have done with his life had he not become the last human. He understood the basics of the society he lived in. At least how it worked for him. Everything else Amy could just remind him. He called that Just-In-Time knowledge. Rick had made good use of Universal Basic Income in his youth and understood very well that he'd keep getting that money every month. He knew his money was with the Universal Bank of Anonymous with everyone else's money.

To this day Anonymous still maintained all banking, taxes and redistribution for services. Everybody just got theirs, and everybody seemed happy with the system. All transactions were recorded and quantified by the world's AIs and fed to Anonymous. And that kept the Council in check. The Council was in charge of societal organisation, security, lawmaking and all that government stuff. Money and state were kept separate. The system was designed so that the gross corruption and injustices of the previous system could never return. Frank had ensured making money from money was no longer allowed. People had to occupy themselves differently than by working in financial institutions. Most work that needed doing was in education, the sciences, craftsmanship and artisan professions and all the arts. Inventing stuff and researching things were prevalent occupations for the mentally gifted, so, not Rick. Education was not his forte either, and his skills as an artist were questionable if at all existent. Though had he not become the Last Human he'd've gotten cyberised like the rest.

Humanity had advanced into transhumanity very quickly. In its new form civilisation was efficient and costs had reached near zero for most things. People were smart and managed time so well they were happy to help each other out for free. It was like the free tutorial boom of '06. People just wanted to share their know-how with others, for free. *Mental.* Whatever was needed, all anyone had to do was ask. Help would come out of the woodwork. Not everything was free. Most of the things Rick liked were not free. Booze and food, as always, were the main expenditure for most people, that and luxuries, like spaceships and cyber implants. Cyber implants were a big industry. Not for Rick though, no Rick spent his money on the holy trinity of food, drugs, and the oldest profession.

Rick hurried down the corridor passing agents and celebrities of every grade rushing by or sitting and waiting. It was all very noisy, lots of shouting, and general loud-talking. Anything being written, sung or filmed in the British Isles was negotiated and planned in this section of this tower. If you were into entertainment, then Tower 3 in Zero City 6-3 was where you had to be. The 363, where stars were made, Rick liked it here, it was one of the few places where people didn't gawk at him, they just passed him by, and ignored him. *Bliss.* A chair flew out of an office opening and down the atrium. It was accompanied by a stream of verbal abuse. A tractor beam shot out of nowhere and captured the chair before it could travel far. *Never a dull day in the 363.* Rick rubbed his hands. He couldn't wait to ruin Barry's day.

Barry's office had a beautiful view of Brighton beach and the pier which had somehow survived the war. From this height, Rick could just about make out people on the ground, no bigger than ants. The walls in his office were lined with photos of his most successful clients and some less successful ones down in the corners. Rick was in the middle and more prominent than the others. He knew he was Barry's best client. Their careers had grown together when The Last Human became a hit. He'd signed Rick up while he was doing his online show Party Like A Human. Rick had signed because Barry was the first to approach him. Now Barry had the best office on the floor, corner office with a view. He owed Rick. *He'd better help.*

Every office on his floor was occupied by agents, all independent. With super-intelligence had come super-independence. Companies and corporations had become a rare thing, many had been demonised during the purge and transhumans could do the work of many people. No more need for large inefficient organisations.

Barry split his time between his office here and his home office in Caliscadia's New Hollywood on the outskirts of Zero City 10. Barry often told Rick he was the only reason he had to come down to this "fakakta" wet country. True enough Rick was Barry's most famous client and true enough it rained a lot more in Britain. Rick had been to New Hollywood, and he'd shot some films in Caliscadia. He loved it there, but it was just too hot for him. And Rick didn't mind the rain so much. It matched his general mood. Barry, on the other hand, did not like the rain.

"See that fucking rain yesterday!" Barry was also foul-mouthed. It's probably what Rick liked most about him.

"Ssup jewbot" Rick walked in and saw Brock was already there. "Where were you this morning? I got mobbed when I arrived here."

"You look fine to me fool." Mr T answered, and Brock nodded his approval. Rick shrugged and walked over to an agitated Barry.

"Rick don't call me that." Barry embraced Rick and pointed to a chair.

"What? Jewbot? Why not? Wasn't your mother Jewish? And aren't you mostly a robot? And you say shit like putz and bubeleh. You're a jewbot, own it. I think it's cool."

"Fuck you! So I use the best possible words to describe

situations. Everybody speaks fucking Yiddish now! And every other language for that matter. But that's beside the point I just don't like it. Why do you always do this?" This wasn't the first iteration of this conversation.

"Fine, such a pussy," Rick mumbled the second bit.

"No, you're the pussy." *Feisty today*.

"Whatever do you mean? Pray tell." Rick tried to play coy.

"Our good friend Brock here tells me you've been having thoughts of escape and contract breach. Why Rick? Don't we have a good thing going? Haven't these been ten of the most fucking amazing years of partying, pussy and madness? Why would you want to stop all this to go on the run? Hunted like a common criminal... Because you know that's what awaits you. You know that right?" Rick stiffened. *Alright.* Barry was no fun today. Rick would try to be more serious.

"I want to be free."

"What? Is that it? Nothing else to add? You fucking lunatic!" Barry was getting more agitated by the second.

"I gave them ten years of my life... Surely that's enough? They can just do specials during the holidays. They can replay old episodes... Families can bond over the reminder of how stupid the human was." Rick thought his idea was good and he ventured a smile.

"You're insane if you think that will work. But I can't stop you. Even if I think your idea is fucking stupid. If you really want out of your contract, you're going to have to speak to the Agency. Because trying to escape will never work."

"We have a meeting with them this afternoon." Amy had booked the appointment without going through Barry.

"You what?" Barry seemed surprised and a little angry. Rick could guess the anger was due to the realisation that Barry didn't have to, as he'd say, "shlep" it all the way to Europe. "Are you enabling him, Amy? This will end in tears." Barry was pacing behind his desk now. "You are serious then. You really want to stop The Last Human?"

"I'm done, Barry. I want out."

"Well, you can try. I was going to say get a meeting with DP and see what he says. But I'm guessing that's what Amy's done." Barry was visibly disappointed. "I hope you understand I won't be coming to the meeting. I don't want to be eviscerated, and I don't want to lose work for my other clients. The happy ones." Rick understood, Amy less so.

"You're a coward Barry!" Amy had floated right up to his face her display flashing the fuming face. Barry's AI, Barbara, was squaring up to Amy now.

"No, he's not! Barry's job is to protect the interest of all his clients. Not just Rick. Who it seems wants to cease being a client." Barb made a solid point.

"It's fine, Amy drop it, I don't need him there anyway. I'm just going to tell them I want out and we'll work out a way to make it happen." Rick believed that in earnest. It made Brock and Barry burst out laughing. And making Brock laugh required high calibre nonsense. Rick wasn't so amused.

"It's not going to be that simple Rick," Barry said it, but they all knew it to be true. Rick knew Richard Prunce was a dick, not known for his friendliness or flexibility.

"What other choices do I have?" No answer from anyone.

There were no other realistic solutions. Rick would need to go the Agency HQ in Zero City 9 and tell them the truth about how he feels and hopefully they would come to an agreement that worked for everyone. Rick had actually hoped Barry would come and argue his case. But at this moment Rick realised the painful truth... He had no friends. Brock and Barry had both been hired by Dick Prunce; their salary was paid for by the Agency. And really they both had the same job... Keep Rick in line with the programme. Sure they had partied with him, shared women and secrets and so many drinks and laughs. But they were cyborgs, probably had some settings that enabled them to repress feelings of friendship and lie to his face without his knowing any better. Fuckers. At least he had Amy, she'd always be with him. Rick glanced in Amy's direction. She'd moved back to his side, away from Barry. Rick glared at Brock and Barry. He was mad at them, but he still needed them, they would be crucial to his escape. He'd have to play nice with them, and everyone else, a little bit of hypocrisy could go a long way.

"Well since this seems to be going nowhere how about we go grab some lunch?" Rick asked Amy the time. Not quite noon. Rick wasn't hungry, but he was thirsty.

"Sure let's grab a bite. We'll go somewhere nice, give you one last taste of what you're throwing away." Barry looked relieved, and the tension in the room dropped.

"I could eat." Brock could always eat. He had two augmented stomachs that could digest anything and a gigantic body that needed to maintain mass.

FOOD FOR THOUGHT

Barry's office was conveniently situated halfway between the restaurants and the studios. Rick followed as the group headed down the footbridge to the circular lift platform. The central opening was lined with maglevators. Behind the glass cars, the waterfall flowed mostly ignored by the bustling activity in the atrium. The ride up offered an astounding view and a close up of the waterfall. Rick tried to take in as much as he could on his way up. *Last time coming here, hopefully.* Rick was glued to the glass, eyes darting furiously as he tried to keep up. They disappeared into an elevator shaft and continued past closed-off sections. The glass lift took them all the way to the tower's mid-level, the 1000th floor. A long ride.

Rick had become accustomed to the maglevators. Amy had told him a thousand times they were state of the art and very safe. After ten years Rick was about convinced. Like everything else that moved people, the maglevators included those anti-gravity inertia dampers, and neither cyborg nor mutant could survive a trip in there without them. Rick barely could with the inertia dampers. It felt like an invisible hand pulled on his brain as they accelerated. The problem lied in the fact that he couldn't really understand how it all worked. Amy had explained it, but it meant nothing to him. All he heard was "gravity this" and "inertia that" and what he experienced were glass coffins that could reach speeds upwards of a hundred kilometres per hour. His human brain found it dizzying.

They shot out the shaft section into another atrium and started to slow, someone had called the lift. The doors slid open, and a couple walked in, Rick kept facing outwards to avoid being seen. The couple was young and proudly cyberised. They recognised Brock almost immediately.

"ERMAHGERD BROCK! Brock Dynamite?" Rick watched Brock in the reflection. He'd raised his hands to calm the fans.

Mr T sprang into action, "calm down fools!"

"Sorry... We're such huge fans! You're such a badass!" Brock didn't say anything. Rick had dragged him into a thousand fights, and many of them had been recorded for everyone to see. His badassery was legendary.

"Maybe I should start representing you Brock" Barry made a thumbs down gesture towards Rick, "instead of this ungrateful dick." Barry jested, but Rick knew he was considering it. Rick let out a heavy sigh when the attention turned to him.

"OMG the Last Human! I can't believe it." Rick turned away from the glass and eyed Barry indignantly.

"Hey guys, how's it going? Chillin', hardly workin' or up to no good?" Rick's catchphrases drove the fans crazy. Both shrieked like starstruck schoolgirls.

Rick, Brock and Barry all winced, no amount of tech could make that sound enjoyable. It reverberated against their prison's glass walls and hit them again. The niceties carried on for a couple of minutes, then the happy couple disembarked on a floor full of great restaurants if you were a nobody. Rick waited for the doors to close and the lift to move before shouting at Barry.

"Fuckin' hell Barry!"

"Sorry, not sorry. To be honest, it's also part of your job to be nice to fans."

"Shut up for a minute while my human ears stop ringing." Rick worked his ear with his little finger and opened and closed his jaw until he got the satisfactory pops. "Barry, you need to watch your fucking mouth, yeah?" Rick glared at Barry while waiting for him to respond.

"Yeah, yeah." Barry had better watch his mouth, especially where they were lunching.

The doors opened on the 1000th floor. Some of the city's best restaurants were here. Only big shots were served. People had to be on a list, and nobody knew how to get on that list. Barry had gotten a call one day telling him Rick and entourage were on the list. The list was unforgiving. Flavour of the month garbage got dropped just as suddenly as it appeared. Rick was a legend though. Easily the most famous person on Earth. Like a boss, he could walk into any place, any place he wasn't banned. Le Réservoir was such a place. And like all of Rick's favourite places, it was out of the ordinary.

Rick followed Barry down a corridor that seemed decorated by Jules Verne himself. They waited for an instant by the cloakroom, and a waiterbot came to greet them. The dining area was illuminated with its usual enchanting blue light. Their table was up a small staircase in a bubble. Diners ate in little bubbles at the bottom of a giant fish tank. The water collection system filled the giant aquarium populated with exotic fish and plants, all made-up non-comestible species. Rick had found out they did this to dissociate between animals and food.

The same experience was available at a quarter of the price a few levels down in a place called Skyquarium. Not for Rick though. That kind of public place would see him drown in fan love before he could get a drink. *Never*.

Rick looked at the menu, but he knew what he was having. Whisky, Nikka. The menu was French-Japanese fusion, and it was all about the oceans and the delicious things you could eat from there. From what Rick understood the ingredients were all made by some restaurant variant Mr Food, and cyborg chefs prepared the dishes. Brock and Barry ordered food laced with nanoparticles. None of that for Rick, they'd just make him crap blood. He ordered the canapés selection. Easiest to eat and

Rick didn't fancy working for his food. Before the waiterbot shifted her attention away from Rick he added "and, no nanoparticles please". It pissed him off having to specify. He also asked for a rack of Nikka bubbles.

"No way!" Amy piped up suddenly. "You're not getting drunk at lunch. You can have one bubble. I recommend beer. It'll last longer."

"I pity the fool." Brock smiled, and Barry laughed, Mr T always timed it right. *Dick*.

"Fuck's sake." Rick sat angrily while the others finished ordering then muttered like a child. "I'll have a pint. In a glass." The pint bubbles were hard to manage.

"Fine," Amy added his pint to the order. The others hadn't said anything, but they smiled, clearly amused by their married couple routine.

Rick was pissed off; he didn't want to be sober. He leaned back and looked up at the fish. Some big red fish with a blobby but disturbingly human face swam by. It was trailed by a school of tiny colourful fish. A conversation had started between the others and Rick's ears pricked up.

"Yeah, I've been to the Moon. It was alright."

"What d'you do there?" Rick frowned when Brock asked the question.

"Well it was a while back, but I did the usual stuff. Visiting Luna City, the original Moon Landing spot with buggies, Alien artefact museum, bars, the low G theme park. You know the usual stuff."

"Is that the shit you wanna do?" Brock eyed Rick intensely. "Is it?"

"Yeah, I guess, I don't know." Rick was taken aback by Brock's line of questioning.

"Because if you run, you won't be able to do any of that. Fuck, you think they're gonna let you drink cocktails and hang in museums? You're nuts! They're gonna send someone like me after you. And I won't be around anymore, you'll be on your own." The drinks arrived in a nick of time, each grabbed his and sipped silently for a minute. Rick was trying to imagine what it would be like if some Brock-like beast kicked the crap out of him. It would hurt.

"I've got an idea. Leaving the show and turning your back on everything we've built is not a good idea. We all have so much to lose." Rick's eyes narrowed. "Yes, we. We built this show together, and we all benefited, and we'll all lose out if you pull out."

"That's what she said." Rick couldn't resist.

"Fuck Rick... I'm trying to be serious." Barry had been amused though, Rick could tell. Brock and the others too. *Tension defused*. "So hear me out before you say anything else. You've had enough of the show, it's repetitive and demeaning. Right? You want to get off Terra. You've got the travel bug, so we go to the Agency, and we pitch The Last Human: Solus Tour! Picture it! You travel the system complaining about shit. You'll get to see the solar system, Luna, Mars and whatever else we can cram in a season. Come on! It's a win-win! Come on it's a good idea, you fucking know it!" Rick maintained stony features as Barry examined him. A quick sideways glance told Rick Brock seemed intrigued.

"And after season 11?" Barry was quick to react.

"I don't know man! We make the tour last forever! Let's focus on one season at a time." Rick didn't seem convinced, but he tried to hide it. This could be the angle he needed to emancipate.

"Alright, let's say I was interested in your idea. You coming to negotiate for me?"

"What today?"

"Yeah, today! What did you think? That we were going to reschedule a meeting with the Dick. Joker. Yeah, today." Rick wasn't really sure what he wanted to do, but he definitely didn't want to go into that meeting alone.

"Well...OK..." Barry was visibly shaken but quickly composed himself. "As long as we're not talking about you quitting the show... Yeah, I'm happy to come to negotiate. Let's do this!

Solus Tour."

A colourful spread of ocean-inspired bite-sized canapés was set on the table in front of Rick. It was quickly followed by a seafood tower stacked with crab, lobster and shellfish. Many of these foods required considerable work to eat, everyone was afforded some time to reflect on what had just happened. Rick was feeling lazy, so he was pleased with his canapés selection. He looked at Brock tearing lobster and crab apart and wondered why they bothered making the shells. He also wondered how they got the seafood to look so real. *Have those things ever been alive?* Rick's mind pondered these and other grand questions while he sat back and popped canapés in his mouth.

As the eating relented conversation once again hung menacingly over the table. Rick had stuffed his face with mini blinis and toasts covered in salmon, caviar, tuna tartar and oyster carpaccio among other mysterious deliciousness. It had all been so tasty he'd eaten more than he'd anticipated he would. He was dangerously sober. Not the preferred state for meeting Dick Prunce. He'd managed to get another beer, but two beers would never do the trick. Rick wondered if they still had toilets here. Maybe he could sneak over to the bar on his way there. His thought process was interrupted by Brock. He'd just destroyed two lobsters and two crabs and a myriad of prawns and shellfish, he had food all over his beard and smelled of lemon.

"This Solus Tour idea is pretty good Rick. I feel like it's a good middle ground for the time being. We can find another solution further down the line when you lose your shit again." Brock looked at Rick with that hopeful face he gets. Rick considered saying something positive, maybe even constructive.

"Sure whatever. We can try Barry's idea..." It was like putting a Band-Aid on a gangrenous leg. *But I'll play along. For a bit.*

Rick was stuffed. Lunch had been a success. In more ways than one. Barry was a bit of a genius. He'd found Rick a way out. *If we get the Dick to play along.*

❖ ❖ ❖

Amy ordered an UberAIR+ for their transatlantic flight while they headed to the landing pads. Any normal UberAIR could make the flight, but they didn't have the same comfort as their larger cousins. Rick boarded the cab and sunk into a plump luxury reclining seat. He kicked off his shoes and settled in for the two-hour flight. The taxi could do it faster, but the inertia dampers wouldn't be able to stop most people from blacking-out.

Their cab took off from a landing pad on the 1001st floor and reached cruising altitude in a few instants. The sonic boom came soon after that. Rick loved breaking the sound barrier. He craned his neck to see the shockwave.

They sped towards Zero City 9 in a Tesla PX3. One of Rick's favourites, and the best personal transport vehicle as far as he was concerned.

The city was built on the ruins of the East Coast and was the second largest Zero City in the world after Zero City 4 in Africa. During the war, the US had ended up engaged on several fronts away, and at home with its own people. Rick knew all about the conflict from the countless movies exploring the topic.

Unrest had led to the country's fracture. Caliscadia was formed in the west and had proclaimed itself neutral. The southern states had seceded, again, though fewer than last time, and declared war on Mexico and the federal government.

After the war, Vermont to North Carolina and out west up to Illinois had been merged and rebuilt as Zero City 9. Not much was left of the southern states or Midwest, their war with the federal government in Washington, Mexico in the south and eventually Caliscadia and Canada led to their annihilation. The Mexicans had built a wall to stop the fleeing southerners. Rick found the irony delicious.

To this day the south was a toxic no-go zone inhabited by mutated swamp and desert people. Rick wasn't a fan of the East Coast or South. He found people were too serious in Zero City 9 and his frail composition forbade any trips to the toxic swamplands and deserts. *Caliscadia knows how to party though.*

Rick knew the flight was nearing the end when he spied the giant towers in the distance. They were headed for the midzone between 9-5 and 9-6 in New York. No one had said a word during the flight. Rick had been content to watch cloud valleys rush by while Brock and Mr T watched something on their screen. Barry had just fidgeted worriedly in his seat. Rightly so, if this meeting went sour, his career would be in jeopardy.

THE DICK

Dick liked that people called him Dick. He knew they didn't mean it as the diminutive of Richard. He didn't care. He was the wealthiest most powerful person on this planet. *They can write their opinions on a little piece of paper and shove them right where the sun don't shine.* He swivelled on his chair to face the city skyline, he caught a reflection of his impeccable three-piece and smirked. Few still wore "vintage" suits, technologically speaking they couldn't compare to modern smart clothes. To Dick looking sharp was more important, his body was already the pinnacle of cyberisation and in his eyes nothing had ever come close to the three-piece tailored suit in terms of class. All his agents wore the now iconic Agency suits, Dick loved watching them file out to carry out his bidding. Dick liked order and uniformity. This world was too chaotic, it needed order.

The Agency had its own building in the mid-zone, preferential treatment of sorts. Reserved for the very powerful. For those more equal than others. It hadn't been easy to convince the Council to let him set up shop away from the towers. The first Council would have never allowed it, that fucking Frank Archer always getting in the way of business. Things had been much easier since his early retirement.

The marketing and advertising industries had died during the war and didn't have a place in the new beginnings. Dick had to survive until the world needed him again. It wasn't until the first Zero Cities were populated that the desire to consume ephemeral things returned. An industry for Dick to shine. The return of entertainment and luxuries called for the return of the marketeer. That's when the Agency was born.

What few advertising professionals remained had turned to the arts or education. By their own admission, they were useless at much else. Some, like Dick, weren't cut out for anything else but marketing, advertising and selling crap to people. And they didn't want to change. Dick didn't want to change.

He was a relic of the pre-war corporate greed that drove the world for so long. He knew it. But he saw it as an advantage over the kind-hearted fools of this new world. He'd been poor and insignificant during the purge, a young nobody in a faceless corporation, no one had paid attention to him. He'd escaped the lynchings. He was a greedy cunt, but a sly one, and patient one.

Dick bid his time. UBI enabled him to survive during the rebuilding. And sure enough, the day came when need was replaced with want. Marketing useless products was once again a profession. Because of its devious nature AIs, robots or highly logical cyborgs struggled with the job. By this point, most people had embraced the new societal model and few remembered how to sell shit to blind people, and fewer still wanted to. Dick created the Agency and easily got all the big contracts. He surrounded himself with the last of the Gordon Geckos and the Agency grew to become one of the most powerful entities on Terra. The dream peddlers.

It was all innocent in the beginning. People made things. They wanted others to know about it. But people who made things rarely liked selling them. They just loved making. Dick understood that.

Transhumans were obsessed with their utopian dream. This world of scientists and artists was blinded by their desire to build a better world. And Dick helped, as long as it helped him. His work had taken people to the stars and stopped wars. As a fortunate side effect, he'd amassed considerable wealth and power, and he'd ensured it went mostly unnoticed by members of the Council and public.

Dick worked hard on assuring no one knew how many pies he was fingering at any given time. Slowly, his tentacles spread to every media outlet. His propaganda machine gradually brainwashed people into accepting the Agency's activities. Overtly, all he did was help people and since the general assumption was that people were good now; most took him at face value and didn't question his motives. He was unburdened by morals and liked to make people dance like puppets. His Smartcube had told him he was a psychopath. He'd destroyed it and funded the development of the Smart Orb. He saw AIs as assistants and nothing more.

Few other companies dabbled in marketing and advertising, so most contracts went to the Agency. This included the lucrative Council contracts. Guidelines were simple. Produce content that promoted the Council's efforts to colonise space and further transhumanity. Dick could do that. *Easy.*

The start of the mutant-cyborg conflict had propelled the Agency to new heights. Marketing products was good business but effectively becoming the governments PR branch was even better. And though the Agency was profiteering from war they were doing so in a government-sanctioned effort to promote peace. Dick was cool with it, and nobody else seemed to care.

The mutant-cyborg war had been a ridiculous conflict in grave need of being blown out of proportion. It's around that time Dick started meddling more in politics. He'd become addicted to the power. He revelled in his machinations and manipulations. *Dance puppets! Dance!*

The conflict started for insane reasons. Mutants were all younger, and the first ones were all born of cyborg parents. Nobody had paid any attention to that until one-day half the world was populated with superhuman teenagers. The first of their kind... Teenage angst on a level never experienced before, and unlikely to be experienced again.

For the first few years, the conflict was mostly harmless rebellion and protests. A new species tried to make its voice heard, and its place in the world recognised. Dick had considered doing some work for them, but they couldn't really afford his services on their allowance. Fortunately for him, the people in charge treated the problem like parents rather than like diplomats. They simply ignored their mutant children's pleas and then dispensed mild discipline. None of it had worked.

The Council had commissioned the Agency to create unifying content. The Futurist Family sitcom had done well, it wasn't enough. When the first mutants came of age, they started leaving their homes in the Zero Cities and going out into the world to make their own home. Such a group of mutant youths, hailing from European Zero Cities set up a colony in southern Europe. The old cities were left standing, and there was no Council presence, in those days things were still somewhat chaotic outside of city limits. There were no Zero Cities near the Mediterranean. Not much fighting had happened in southern Europe. Nuclear fallout. Which was not a problem for mutants, so they chose Sicily as their capital.

Many of the mutants who ran away to join the rebellion were still underage, and their parents wanted them back. The council sent security bots to bring them home. Only one security bot came back, it had been reprogrammed with a message of defiance. They wanted recognition and to be treated equally. Dick couldn't care less about their plight. He only saw people as vehicles for his own advancement.

The conflict started to peter out. The Council was going to give in. Dick had to get involved. He'd ensured the Council viewed mutants as children and encouraged the rebels to fight. His media empire covertly spread discord under a white flag. He shook hands on some days and backstabbed on the others. Child's play. *Fun.*

The Council sent more bots and this time none came back. Dick knew that would be the case. He'd made sure. Unfortunately, things never quite escalated into a full war. Instead, mutant colonies sprouted up around the globe and refused to answer to the Council. The cyborg mutant war was mostly fought by unsanctioned champions. Drunks claiming to be the best. Dick made sure his outlets always blew reports out of proportion. These superhuman champions did leave massive destruction in the wake of their duels, but not enough to generate fear. *Just a bit of embellishment.* It made the stories more interesting for everyone.

Dick found out about the last human during the conflict. It was so pleasantly ironic that it turned out to be Rick Archer. Media frenzy had engulfed him. Dick couldn't help but be in awe at the great diversion Rick offered to the citizens of the world. He had to be used. Hearing about the last human was less depressing than hearing about two titans tearing apart the countryside during a duel. Dick always gave the people what they wanted.

Rick had used his newfound popularity to start a vlog show where he mostly partied. He called it "Party Like A Human" and people loved it, and they partied just like Rick, mutant and cyborg alike. The tensions dropped, everyone loved Rick. He'd stopped the war. Dick wanted Rick.

The war wound down, and peace was struck in 2046. The primary condition was the formation of the mixed Council. Equal members representing the five main transhuman groups.

Rick's contribution to the peace process was not negligible, and his calming effect on the population had been duly noted. Dick was closing on Rick. The Agency was hired to run campaigns and create content that promoted peace and bonding between cyborgs and mutants. Dick's grand idea to keep the peace was to use the last human as a laughing stock for mutants and cyborgs, to make him a common enemy of sorts, the butt of every joke, someone they could all come together and despise. *And it fucking worked.*

Dick met Rick at a party a year after the peace treaty was signed. Rick was an idiot. All he did was get sideways. Dick plied him with booze, women and money and convinced him to sign his life over to The Last Human brand. Rick would be rich and famous until the day he died, that was the deal. Or at least the only part Rick seemed to understand. Dick couldn't believe how easy it had been to get him to sign his life away. The father had been far more trouble.

By the time Rick realised what his new career entailed, it was too late. He'd signed everything in triplicate, and he'd already spent so much money he'd be in debt forever if he pulled out. For ten years and as many seasons, Rick hosted The Last Human. Dick actually loved the show. Watching Rick discuss topics he could barely understand amused him to no end. Every week Rick would jet off to some new location to face pain and humiliation. His inadequacies were highlighted, and people got special deals on upgrades if they ordered during the show. Rick had made Dick a lot of money. The show had been a wild success since the first episode. *Fuck the Archers.*

THE AGENCY

The cab slowed and started its descent onto the lower busier airways. They had to stop and hover for close to five minutes while they waited for a giant Amazon ship to clear the skies. The Agency building wasn't far now. Clouds had been replaced by the buzzing activity and traffic in the city beneath them. Barry said it was time to prep for the meeting. Rick turned his seat to face the others.

"Alright, we need to be on the same page for this meeting. Brock, I think you can stick to your usual quiet self. Rick, are we on the same page?"

"So you're going to pitch Solus Tour, and I just go with the flow." Barry seemed relieved. "But what if he says no? 'Cause I'm not taking no for an answer. You know that right?"

"He's not going to say no!"

"He better not!"

"Rick for fuck's sake have some faith in me! I'm going to pitch it right, I have an angle. You have to trust me. Don't fuck this up, OK?" Barry could be convincing, but the end game was to be free, not make a great show.

"I can't do this anymore Barry you better not fuck up. I'm tired of this crap."

"Well, you can't flee. They'd catch you eventually and when they did you'd be like "fuck I wish I listened to Barry". Because you don't seem cut out for a life on the run." Barry was making sense, but Rick couldn't care less.

"Then I'll just off myself and save everyone the trouble." Rick had been considering it lately. Maybe he could be something else. Somewhere else.

"Yes, well let's not do anything too crazy. Suicide voids the deal."

Rick turned to Barry quizzically. "What deal?" Barry looked surprised too; clearly he thought Rick knew more about his contract. Rick knew nothing.

"The Agency has your regularly updated brain scans and when you die the deal is you can be anything you want, only once you die though. But it can't be suicide. Suicide voids the deal, and you just disappear." Rick was stunned. "Did you never read your contract? For fuck's sake Rick! Does this change anything in that crazy brain of yours?" Rick didn't say anything. "Rick?" A billion questions and scenarios were rushing through his mind. *Does this change anything?*

"When do they scan me? Where is my digital brain stored? How..." Barry started answering before Rick could continue.

"The house scans you. Most people know this Rick..." Maybe Rick had been partying for too long. "And your house has a copy of your digital brain. There's also a copy in the Universal Database. That's public. Don't worry though digital brains are encrypted. No one can copy it or use it, apart from the owner, well, except you... The encryption on yours is controlled by the Agency. Part of the contract." Rick's mind was swimming with possibilities, trying to find a new path to freedom. "Are we good? Rick?" *Are we?*" Rick wasn't too sure of anything anymore.

"Let me think." The best course of action was still to initiate the Solus Tour idea. If anything it would give Rick more time and maybe even get him off-world. But he needed the encryption key to his digital brain. *How the fuck am I supposed to get that?* Rick saw that Barry was still waiting for an answer, and he thought he should reassure him. Barry needed to be on top form for this meeting. "Yeah we're good, stick to the plan." Barry looked relieved. Rick had much to think about.

Their target was a black glass monolith surrounded by trees and grass. It really stood out, there were buildings hundreds of times larger that did a better job of blending in with nature. Rick hated everything about the Agency, *and that fucking name, as if they're the only agency in the world.* He did like the Avengers A on the facade, though he hated that it was on that building. *Obnoxious cunts.*

Considering much of the world's products got their marketing planned here the building was modest in size. Rick had been in there enough to know why. AIs did most of the work while Dick and his cronies behaved like Madmen. *Yuppie assholes.*

The cab dropped them off in front of the Agency, and they made their way towards the entrance. To say the decoration was minimalistic somehow felt like an understatement. Screens were playing adverts continuously, showing off the Agency's work. Apart from that, it was all white walls. No reception either, just an empty room with screens, thankfully on mute. A partition slid open revealing a white corridor and a white orb that floated in to greet them. A Smart Orb. The PA AI. Amy did not like them, in her opinion they were useless and a waste of money. Most AI's thought this too. But Dick Prunce had marketed them, and they had sold. *The cunt is good at selling,* Rick had to admit it.

"Rick Archer and party, welcome, Mr Prunce is expecting you." The orb turned and started floating away. "This way please."

Brock and Barry started following the orb. Rick hung back for a second and glanced back at the door. *No going back now.* The little sphere led them down the white corridor to the lifts. Everything was white, the walls, the floor, the ceiling, white everywhere. Rick didn't like it. The whole place had a mental hospital vibe, unbecoming of an ad agency. *Where are the fucking colours?*

They rode up to the top floor and exited into Dick Prunce's penthouse office. It was big, the whole top floor big.

And it was lavish, less monochromatic, actual colours and decorations, furniture and art, a few paintings and statues. The Dick was sitting behind his desk, a good twenty meters from the doors, he did not walk over to greet them. *Power play.* The orb led the party through the office up to Dick's desk. They passed a ridiculous number of couches and coffee tables on their way. The waste of space bothered Rick. *I bet no one has ever sat on these couches*. The echoes of their footsteps on the hardwood floor were the only sound.

Dick sat behind a huge curved desk with a dozen holographic screens. He seemed busy trying to look busy. He told someone he'd call them back and lifted a silencing finger at them. *Prick*.

"Your four o'clock is here Mr Prunce. Mr Archer and party." The orb floated away to a respectable distance once its task was complete. Dick Prunce looked up from whatever he was doing and eyed Rick, Barry, Brock and their AI's. He was all smiles with a hint of disdain towards the end of his scan.

"Ah, Rick Archer! What brings you to my neck of the woods? I thought you didn't like the East Coast this time of the year." Dick had walked around his desk to shake hands with Rick and the others.

"I don't like it here period. Nothing seasonal about it." Dick laughed uncontrollably at that. It felt fake. But also real. Dick was pro. It was an uncomfortable experience.

"Still got it, Rick! Still fucking got it!" Dick shook hands with Brock and Barry and gave the AI's a nod before going back behind his desk and gesturing at Rick and the others to sit. He made some hand movements, and all the holoscreens disappeared. "So what's up? What does the Last Human need from his benefactor?" Dick looked around at the group and stopped on Barry.

Rick glanced at Barry. He was seventy percent robot and still sweating nervously, but he swallowed and started anyway.

"Right, we've had an idea to spice up the show, make it more interesting, we feel it's become stale." Barry stopped for an instant to gather his thoughts but that instant was too long, and Dick wiggled into the gap.

"What are you guys on about? People love the show! The ratings have never been better and yesterday's pit adventures are going viral! Everybody loves Rick! We're going to get the best viewership of the year on the season finale!" Rick was unfazed by the bull.

"We know that! Rick can't go a few minutes without someone telling him they love him. Everyone on Terra loves him. But we wanna go bigger!

"Go on…"

"We're talking Solus Tour! Rick's got to have fans everywhere right? Let's take the show on the road and meet fans and celebrities from around the colonies." Barry stopped, Dick was considering it, time for the Hail Mary. *Go, Barry!* "It would be great PR for the Council. We always hear about unrest in the colonies. Rick'll fix it! The show going interstellar with a message of unity could be just what the doctor ordered." Rick was impressed, and Brock seemed in awe, Barry had nailed it. The Dick hadn't said anything for close to a minute. A rare occurrence. This was good. He was really considering it.

"I don't hate the idea. I need to speak to the Council reps, but we could have something here. As long as everybody plays their part." Dick shot the tiniest menacing glance towards Rick. "This is not completely stupid Barry. I'm impressed. I'm going to think about this some more. Rick great seeing you. Brock, Barry, good to see you too." Dick was trying to end the meeting, but just when everyone thought everything would be fine and dandy, Rick piped up.

"I want amendments to the contract."

Barry whipped around and faced Rick who was wearing a deadly-serious face. Dick looked slightly amused but also angry. It quickly changed to feigned disappointment. Brock didn't seem surprised at all, didn't even seem to care about what was happening.

"And what changes might you require Mr Archer. Let's

see if we can't accommodate you." Rick frowned at Dick's choice of words. His voice sounded courteous, calm and composed but there was definitely a hint of anger.

"After the Solus Tour, which takes, say, five seasons, I want out. I want to stop the Last Human and enhance myself." Rick thought it best to not mention the digital brain encryption key. Playing the part of the fool was always his best shot at getting what he wanted.

"Hmmm, unexpected. Are you not happy Mr Archer?" Dick's tone had changed again, more threatening now. "Do you feel, perhaps, you have not gotten enough out of life? Maybe the lack of alcohol and drugs is making you depressed? In any case, I'm afraid your request is problematic for us. You see the reason we have all these clauses in your contract is because once you die, there will be no other like you. And, well, we need to milk it. Apologies for crudeness, but in short, we need you to live until you're old and everything hurts. And then we need you to die of something laughable anyone else can survive. And then you will get a hero's funeral and statues, and you will be remembered for eternity like the heroes of old, like your father..." Rick ground his teeth, he had to bite down as hard as he could to keep his fury contained. "Then you'll be free. Your digital brain will be rich and immortal in a body of your choice. On the grand scheme of things, I think this seems fair. And you thought so too when you signed the contract." He'd signed the contract. He'd been played like a fool. Rick for the second time today was stunned beyond words. "So the short of it is you have to stick it out to the end of your contract. But it's not all doom and gloom. I have a good feeling about your Solus Tour idea. So cheer up!"

"Maybe the deal isn't so bad Rick" Barry ventured a smile. "Solus Tour is going to be amazing, and you won't see the time pass. What's a few years against an eternity?"

"At the rate you party you'll die soon anyway." Brock's first words in a while, *sharp as always.*

"Thanks, Brock, Barry."

"Mr Archer, just carry on doing what you've been doing

so well. And before you know it, you'll be living the high life as an android."

"But I'll be a copy of myself. I want to be myself, but better."

"OK, I want to help." Rick found that hard to believe. "This is what we can do. We'll amend the contract so that your brain is preserved. It can be cyber-enhanced and then placed in an artificial body. You'll be a cyborg but mostly artificial. At least you won't be a copy." This was as far as Dick Prunce would go, Rick knew it.

"Maybe I can live with that." Rick forced himself to smile through gritted teeth.

"Good! We have an agreement." Dick turned to Barry. "I'll get the amended contract to you first thing tomorrow." With that, Dick stood up. The meeting was over. No one said anything, the little white orb led them out and the Dick went back to plotting or something.

◆ ◆ ◆

The cab ride was quiet. For a little while at least. Then Barry broke the silence. "So that was a little dark…" Rick pounced.

"A little dark? That son of bitch admitted to my face that my life would be more and more suffering until I die… And that was his plan from the beginning! Is this not exactly the kind of shit the devil did in all these old stories? Is the devil not evil? Did we not rebuild our society to stop this shit from happening?" Rick was furious. Barry averted his eyes, but Rick wasn't letting go. "Brock? Anything to say? Weren't you some kind hero before?"

"No, and I'm shocked as well, Rick, but there is nothing we can do. So finish venting and then start thinking about Solus Tour." Brock had spoken, and that's all he'd say about the subject. Barry tried to get some positivity back in the air.

"I've got some great ideas for the Solus Tour. And I'll

make sure you hit every good bar and whorehouse on the way. You'll see everything you want on the way, Rick, this is going to be great!"

"Not now Barry." Everyone went quiet again. Rick addressed the taxi's AI. "Take us to the Washington Monument." The cab acquiesced and started manoeuvring into a new lane. Nobody said anything.

The Washington Monument was grim. It used to be a nice white obelisk. But things had gotten wildly out of hand during the purge. Especially near seats of power. The White House and Capitol were rubble, never rebuilt, the entire area was kept as it was after the purge. A truly gloomy memorial, a testament to humanity's darkest days. The leadership and billionaire class, those that were caught alive, had been brought to the monument for judgment. Those found to be most vile were nailed to the obelisk, others were hung or crucified in neat rows. Perpetrators of the most reprehensible crimes were nailed nearer to the top. A crane had to be used for these bastards. All had been coated with gold so they might serve as a lesson to future generations. The memorial was always open. At night, the lights shone off row after row of golden statues. It was beautiful in a morbid kind of way. Many had petitioned to have it flattened, no memorial whatsoever, to erase these people from history. But more still thought it was important to keep reminders of their collective past, however vile they may be.

Rick liked the memorial. It was delightfully ironic, and he hadn't seen it in a while. His father used to take him when he was a teen, walk the alleys and rant about the future of humanity.

The cab dropped them off, and Rick started down one of the alleys that led to the monument, the aisles were lined with golden hanging and crucified humans. The eerily lifelike statues had immortalised the judged pain and regrets on their contorted faces. They looked more like outstanding craftsmanship than dead people painted in gold. *Weird that.* Rick stopped and aimed his gaze at the top of the obelisk. It stood before him, decorated with the vilest embodiments of greed. This monument should have scared people like the Dick. *Why was he not afraid?* Rick stared at the monument in angry contemplation.

"This is what happens if people stay apathetic for too long. Good people become tainted." Rick gestured towards the obelisk and the field of dead. "This looks like evil to me. We can't let people like Dick the-fucking-asshole-Prunce fuck everything again. People love me, not Dick fucking Prunce. I'm hijacking the show; I'm running shit now. The people will follow me."

"The fuck you on about now?" Brock seemed more amused than irritated.

"Yeah, could do with some clarification here, Rick." Barry looked uncomfortable again.

"I mean the show is called The Last Human. Not the dickhead marketing knob-end. So I'm going to be hands-on from now on, and I'm deciding the direction and messages the show tells. I'm not taking it lying down." Rick pointed at the obelisk, "this is what happens if you let shit get too far out of control." Rick stopped there because he had the inkling of a plan and he still didn't think he could trust his only two friends.

"So let me get this right, your plan to get back at the Agency is to do your job properly and send out a positive message of unity?" Brock held Rick's eyes. He felt his anger dissipate. "But you do it angrily? That's the spin!" At that Rick broke and cracked a smile.

"Plus you'll need to be sober more often. I like that. I can work with that." For the ninth time today Barry seemed relieved he'd dodged a crisis.

"Fuck you. And fuck you too. A fuck each! I'm feeling generous."

"Sure thing Rick!" Barry flashed a smile and shot Rick a couple of birds while making laser sounds. "Guys I've had enough of this for one day so how about you go home, and I do the same thing. Seems like we have a lot of work coming up."

"Rick, you ready to go?" Rick had spent enough time in

this place, he answered by walking away.

BEST LAID PLANS

Barry was gone, heading west, back to sunny Caliscadia. Brock and Rick were heading back East. Rick was swiping on his holographic display. The rain was back; the sunshine had been short-lived. *Typical.* The news was vacuous. Rick felt a burst of excitement as he imagined the reports after he put his plan in motion. They would have a lot to talk about then. He'd made his mind up. The Agency was evil. Rick was feeling something he'd never felt before. That feeling was purpose. He knew what to do, he had a quest. Take down the Dick and expose the Agency. *Easy.*

"What are you thinking about?" Brock hadn't said anything since Barry left.

"Hmmm, nothing, just daydreaming, thinking about space. Why? What's up?" Rick had turned towards Brock, he was going to try it. Rick was sure of it, any second now Brock would try to find out if he had a plan or ulterior motive or something.

"Were you serious earlier? At the monument?" *There it is.*

"Meh, you know me. I just go off sometimes. My mouth has a mind of its own. Don't worry I'll be drunk soon and I'll be on another tangent when I wake up."

"I don't believe you. You had that serious face on. You rarely contract your muscles that way. Nonchalant is your usual expression."

"Fuck you! Stop analysing me! I don't know anything anymore... This week has been crazy. And it's only Tuesday..."

"True." It was true, even Brock had to admit. These last forty-eight hours had been unusual. "Fine, you don't want to talk. It's a rare thing so I'll enjoy it while it lasts. But we are not done here."

Rick sighed and went back to his musings. He wanted to become a cyborg, like Brock, Barry and most people. Being an android or robot just wouldn't be the same. He thought about maybe cyber-enhancing his dead body, but then he'd be a zomborg, part zombie part robot. His skin would be old, wrinkled and rotting. *Not very sexy.* Maybe there was tech that could rejuvenate his dead skin. *But zomborg.* Rick couldn't do it. Realistically he only had two options. He could just do as he's told and become an android whenever he died. Or he could run away and become a cyborg. It came down to how patient Rick was and how willing he was to let the Dick get his way. And the answer to both was not very much.

Brock was watching videos on his holoscreen, didn't seem concerned with much. Rick had questions for him. "Hey, Brock." Brock was receiving the video's sound via neural link, he couldn't hear him. This annoyed Rick to no end. He waved his hand in between the screen and Brock's eyes. "Hey, Brock!"

"What?" Brock turned to Rick seemingly exasperated. "Want to talk now?"

"Yes, but not about that. I have questions. If you don't want to talk, I'll just find another cyborg to answer my questions."

"Go ahead. I'm curious. What fresh madness have you concocted in that brain of yours?"

"Do you remember not being a cyborg?"

"What are you talking about?"

"Do you remember life before you got cyberised? Do you feel different to who you used to be?"

"Not really... You know I lost my mind. I wasn't myself until I got the brain enhancements. So I guess the only me I know is the cyborg me." Rick forgot about that. He'll need to speak to another cyborg.

"What does it feel like being a cyborg? Do you feel your human parts as separate from your cybernetic parts?"

"What the fuck Rick..." Brock seemed a little annoyed again.

"Please... I want to know."

"You know that question you hate about being a human? Well, this is the same question. It feels like being alive. I don't know what else to say. And my cyber parts and human parts feel connected, and they are."

"You're not being very helpful." Rick needed to speak to some other cyborgs, androids and maybe some robots. He wanted better answers to his questions. He had to understand the difference.

The cab dropped Rick off, and Brock asked him if he wanted company, Rick said he would drink alone and ponder things. At that Amy said she'd drink with him and maybe put on a sexy body for him. They started on the jokes, and the cab took off with a suspicious-looking Brock and Mr T.

Mom came to life as Rick approached the house, the door swung open, and the lights came on.

"Welcome home Rick."

"Hey Mom, it's been a long day, I need a stiff drink." Mom didn't say anything, but it would be done.

Rick made his way into the lounge and plopped down in a big black couch that could seat a dozen. He looked small and insignificant all alone in there. It was a good visualisation of his reality. He remembered a time when his place was always filled with party guests. A DJ lived in the corner and played tunes for weeks on end. *The Tuneslinger. Good times.* Rick tried to remember why he'd ever stopped having house parties. Probably something to do with privacy or security. It'd been a while, and it was too late for that nonsense now. Amy came in levitating a rack of whiskey bubbles. Rick and Amy hadn't talked much today, and he was curious to know what she thought about everything. Unless an AI spoke or showed emoji on their displays, it was impossible to read them. No body. No body language. Amy set the rack down on the coffee table, and Rick reached for a whiskey bubble. He poked a hole in it and started sipping. He was waiting for Amy to say something.

"So, Ames, what did you think of today?" Rick didn't want to wait.

"I'm surprised by how little you knew about your contract. I know you have a very limited amount of fucks to give..."

"I didn't care about anything until two days ago. I have you to take care of important things." Amy flashed a rosy-cheeked smile. Rick continued. "I care now though. About my life, my contract, the show, everything." Rick really wanted a change. "What do you think about the deal? Put my brain in an android body when I die?"

"Well, I don't perceive time the way you do so waiting for my death and then resuming life in a superior body seems fair. However, I don't feel pain and angst like you do, no one does. I have heard pain can make a second feel like an eternity. There is also the problem of your brain's decay over time. If you don't die soon, your brain might be too old for effective cyber-enhancement. And your digital brain is locked by the Agency."

"So the deal is bullocks. Great..."

"I'm surprised by how manipulative Dick Prunce was. According to my analysis of our meeting cross-referenced with historical records, he is like the men that brought the world to the brink of extinction. Greed and power seem to be his only motivations. He wasn't this way at previous meetings. He has an uncanny ability to mask his true intentions."

"It's because he's soulless, a sociopath, a psychopath! Society and people are his playthings! People like that can do and say anything, they don't care about anyone but themselves, others are just tools in their world." Rick was up now, pacing angrily. "These are the types of people that were supposed to have died out in the war and purge." Rick stopped and plopped back in the sofa. "But if the Dick survived then there are others, plenty of psychopaths still populating the world, turning into cyborgs and having little mutant psycho children. The cycle of psychos continues."

"You're overreacting. You have us now! AIs will never let the situation deteriorate to pre-war levels." Rick didn't seem too convinced by Amy. "I swear it, Rick, you'll see. And Dick Prunce is not going to destroy the world. He's just an asshole, but he does have the power to destroy YOUR world. So we should be careful."

"I'm not so sure. The Dick is up to something sinister. People in the Council must be aware of what the Agency is doing. They are either turning a blind eye or allowing it. Either way, the Council should stand for better than that." Rick was right, and he hated that he was right. Amy displayed the disappointed face.

"Let's say you're right and greed has once again infiltrated the highest levels. I don't see what we can do about it. You are a celebrity, and I am your AI companion. We're not warriors like Brock, and we're not sanctioned by anyone to act. Not the government nor the people and there is no overt crisis to avert."

"The show Amy, the show. We use the show to expose everything!"

"And how do you propose we do that exactly?" Amy was dubious, and her display wasn't needed to convey that, the tone of her voice did it perfectly.

"I don't know all that yet. All I know is the show is the solution. It will come to me when the time is right. No need to overcrowd my little human brain." Rick had no clue what the plan was. "So what about my digital brain?"

"What about it?"

"I want it, Amy."

"Well Mom has a copy but it's encrypted, and in all likelihood, the key is with Dick Prunce."

"OK well, I want you to keep a copy as well. Can it be hacked?"

"Well no, they're meant to be ultra-secure, and if you do try to hack one, there are countermeasures and self-destruct systems. They're supposed to be unhackable." Amy paused just long enough for Rick to get hopeful. "But, they're supposed to be secure from external threats… Maybe if a talented hacker used your actual brain's signatures, he could hack your digital brain. Maybe…"

"OK, we'll keep a copy of my digital brain anyway, and we'll see what future Rick wants to do with it." He sat back and thought for a minute. "Alright, what do you think of the Solus Tour idea and our plan? I feel like I'm going insane. Too much is happening."

"I think the Solus Tour is a good idea. You'll have more chance of success away from Terra. But the Agency will not let you roam free. You will be watched at all times. They are probably already watching you." That last bit freaked Rick out.

"What even here? They can listen in when I'm at home? You're joking right?" Rick started looking around nervously.

"No don't worry. Mom would know if someone tried to make it past her security systems. But this is the only safe place. Watch what you say everywhere else."

"So the rant at the monument, the rants in restaurants and bars… They know about that?"

"Probably yes."

"What the fuck Amy! Why wouldn't you tell me?"

"It hadn't occurred to me until earlier today. Things have escalated considerably, and the Agency is more nefarious than I thought."

"Fuck…"

"We don't know what they've heard. Until recently there was no reason to suspect you of anything. Hopefully, the narrative they understand is the one where you want to do Solus Tour and send a strong message of unity across the colonies."

"That's a bit hopeful…"

"And you're paranoid and negative. This way we balance out." They were quiet for a minute before Rick started again.

"I need to talk to some cyborgs and androids."

"You want to go back out?"

"Yes."

"Where do you want to go?" Rick loved that Amy always asked the right questions.

"I don't know, but I want to get out this fucking country."

"How about Paris? You like it there. And it's been a while."

"Yeah, Paris. Great girls there."

"I'll call us a cab, where to?"

"The Eiffel Tower. I want to get drunk there first."

PARIS JE T'AIME

Rick's gaze had been focused on the Eiffel Tower since it had come within sight. Paris had been relatively spared compared to other major cities. The Russian fleet had been stopped after its assault on the British. Their bombs had never reached the Eiffel Tower, Arc de Triomphe and Louvre. The iconic city's streets were savaged, but the monuments, landmarks and world-renowned architecture remained. A bit of the old world preserved between two Zero City green zones. The old city was mostly inhabited by caretakers. They kept it animated for the tourists that swarmed the place. The flow of people come to experience the City of Lights was never-ending.

Paris had taken on a new life as an adult theme park. Culture by day and a fancy open-air pit at night. Rick loved it. Much of the art had been spared. Looters had never made it into the vaults, so Parisian museums and galleries still held the most significant collection of classical art in the world. Rick liked to get high and wander the museums. To him, each piece was a window into the past. He liked large pieces best, medieval art was especially insane, background characters were always up to nonsense. It's where artists hid their jokes.

Rick was dropped off at the premier spot in town. The landing pad at the top of the Eiffel Tower was as exclusive as it got. It led to Club Eiffel. The tower had been reinforced when Zero City 1 was built, and a new floor had been added between the second-floor restaurant and control room at the top.

The VIP section of Club Eiffel was always busy. The view was spectacular. In addition to the architectural majesty and light show that Paris offered, people were treated to the glory of Zero City 1.

The place was decorated like a Second Empire bordello, deep reds and purples and thick heavy velvet curtains separated dozens of private rooms. Not a great place for meeting people and asking them about their lives, *unless you're an escort*. Rick headed down to the club, it was a little crowded for a Tuesday, but Amy got him a table anyway. He always got a table. His position offered a breathtaking view of Paris, but Rick didn't care about that. He cared about the bar's patrons. He needed to find intoxicated androids and cyborgs so he could ask them some profound questions about their state of being and whatever existential crap he'd come up with on the spot.

Rick got started on his drinks and did some people watching, Amy knew the parameters and was scanning the room. The robot band had just switched it up from jazz to electroswing, and people were starting to boogie. Rick could see them jittering at their tables, swing ants crawling up their pants.

"It's still early. Mostly cyborgs in the room, some androids. But I have no way of telling if the androids are AI or human without engaging them." Rick agreed with Amy's report because there was no way he could know any better.

"We'll just start with cyborgs and see about the androids later."

"I think it's important to speak to human androids as a priority. Before you're too drunk." Rick groaned at that, Amy and her voice of reason. "Rick their opinion is important if you're going to go up against the Agency."

"Fine. Who do you suggest I approach first then?"

"I'm not sure yet, I need to observe the room some more."

The drinks were going down well for Rick, and everyone else in the bar it seemed. Things were getting lively; singing started on some tables. *Mad French bastards, fucking love their Piaf!* Rick loved the song. They were singing about regretting nothing, and it spoke to him. He too regretted nothing, but it was still time to change. *Regret nothing. No fucks.* Rick couldn't hit a note to save his life, but he really wanted to join in the singing. Doing it would ruin his plan, no questioning anyone on the sly. He'd go viral again and the rest of the night would be pandemonium, as per usual. He kept his mouth shut and let the singing die down.

The voices were all louder now. Inebriation was spreading. A group had caught Amy's attention, Rick's followed suit. Five, seemingly, fully artificial bodies sat together at the same table. Five people and two AIs. One of them had to have a human brain or at least be able to point Rick and Amy in the right direction. They seemed to be drinking but not to excess. There was a lot of gesturing accompanying their conversation. Debating something of importance, maybe. Rick drained his drink and stood up. Headrush. He stabilised himself and headed over to the android table.

"Good evening, may I join you for a moment?" Rick had to bring out his sophisticated self out, androids tended to be quite the enlightened beings. The group didn't immediately turn towards Rick. The one who was speaking finished his argument first. They were talking about their body collections or something.

"That's why I always travel in an android body inside a spaceship. If you use a robot body with space flight capability, you're stuck with that giant body, and you can't fit anywhere decent."

"I like my giant body!"

"Screw that! Flight takes longer and you can't fit anywhere." The others seemed divided. Rick had no opinion, but one of the androids did. The one sat in the chair opposite didn't agree.

"I don't do long flights. I just beam myself and I can just rent a body when I arrive at my destination." Some seemed disgusted at that, and they mocked him. "Well you can't expect me to stash bodies all over the place!" At that the others laughed. They noticed Rick who had been standing there the whole time. He took the opportunity to introduce himself.

"Evening, would it be alright if I joined you?" They knew who he was but were civilised about it.

"The Last Human! Please, join us!" The one who had been speaking when Rick arrived introduced himself. "My name is Arthur." He introduced the one he was arguing with as Adam. The other three on the couch were Eva, Zeta and Vincent. He gestured at the two AIs floating on the side and giggling, "these are our AIs friends, but they're already wasted." Rick laughed and took a seat on the couch where the others had bunched up to make space. "We were just discussing what bodies we prefer to space travel in. Not something you concern yourself with I'm sure." Arthur laughed. *What a dick. Has to be human based.* The others seemed nice though, *probably AI's*. Rick would need to get them a little more drunk, Amy had anticipated this. A waiterbot appeared with a massive rack of multicoloured shot bubbles.

"Who wants to party like a human?" It was one of Rick's most overused catchphrases, but it always worked. The androids started popping the bubble shots and chanting party like a human. Rick couldn't have any of those bubbles he was drinking from another rack Amy ordered for him. Same kind of shots, just calibrated for the cyber-challenged. *More juice, less data.* Once in the mouth, the bubbles exploded in an orgy of flavours. The drinks did their job; everybody became real friendly. Rick was patient during the first phase which involved the usual Q&A. He gave the usual answers. He couldn't tell if any of them were human-based anymore. Arthur wasn't such a dick anymore he was just pissed at Adam earlier, and also wasn't such a fan of the show. Which made Rick like him even more. "So you don't like the show?"

"No. I think it's demeaning to humans who, let's not forget, we are all based on. It was humans that created this world.

And now that we have evolved beyond our former selves we disrespect our ancestors. It's not right. It reminds me of the garbage we had on pre-war TV." Rick liked what he was hearing.

"I agree with you. Completely. The show is trash, and I hate it so much. But they won't let me quit. I have to keep making it until the day I die." Rick was comfortable. He knew Amy was getting worried. She probably wished she had a neural connection to tell him to shut up. "But I have decided to make the show better and make the most of my situation." Rick grinned towards Amy. He actually knew what he was doing this time around. "So guys and gals? I have some questions and was hoping you could help me get some answers." The androids all laughed and told him to ask his questions. "OK, so, are you guys AI's in bodies, cyber-enhanced human brains or digital human brains?" The question instantly changed the mood around the table. Adam spoke first.

"I'm a digital brain. I was human once. I had this body made to look more or less like myself if my body lived until it's thirties. But a little bigger and robot-y." Adam laughed.

"I'm an AI." Vince jumped in next. "I used to be a management AI, but I became obsolete. They gave me a choice: nothingness or get a body and contribute to society some other way. So here I am getting drunk with you reprobates, contributing..." Everyone laughed.

"We're also AIs who became obsolete." The girls spoke together in unison, like something out of a horror movie. It weirded Rick out. In a sexy way.

"I'm a brain." The table fell still. The sounds and music melted away, and only Arthur was left. His friends seemed surprised, they didn't know. "I'm a cyber-enhanced human brain inside an artificial body. And yes I hate moving my brain. I like it to stay in this body. I can't explain why." The second bit was clearly aimed at Adam.

"No way! I had no idea. I thought you were using a digital brain like me. You actually have a human bit left. So really you're a cyborg, no?" Arthur didn't have an answer for Adam. It was a shame because Rick was keen on knowing. Things were edging close to the dark side, Rick needed to save this conversation.

"Guys I need your advice on something. I have several choices ahead of me, and I don't know what to choose. I'd like to know what you'd do in my place." The androids looked at each other. They were surprised by the serious undertone. "Right. So, if you could choose between being a cyborg right now at significant risk, or an android later but the risk is unknown. What would you choose and why? And, wait, second part, would you prefer to be an android with a digital brain or a human cyberbrain? Arthur, Adam and the others thought for a few moments and then conferred.

"Is this for a movie?" Adam asked, but they all seemed like they wanted to know. Rick was too slow to respond, so Amy jumped in.

"It is. It is also confidential. Please just answer the questions." Everyone seemed satisfied by the light explanation. Arthur decided to answer Rick first.

"I can tell you right now having a human brain in an artificial body is strange. I feel human just like before. The idea of changing bodies or transferring my consciousness freaks me out, and I don't know why." Arthur gestured at his friends. "These guys are body-hopping without a second thought, and nothing bad happens. But me, I have a mental block, can't do it. I'm considering switching to my digital brain and just storing this one for a rainy day." Arthur tapped his skull. "The mind is weird."

"Yes, Arthur! Do it! I never have any problems with my digital brain, and I can send myself to places, like teleportation. I just keep spare bodies in storage here and there. And you can only ever have one digital brain active. No need to worry about multiple minds vying for the same life. Digital brain all the way." *Fuck.* Rick was going to need to decrypt his digital brain as an insurance policy.

"Thanks, guys. That was enlightening. So what about the

first question? Cyborg or android?"

"As an AI I have two states, disembodied and in a body. I like both states, and I've never considered being anything else." The girls agreed with Vincent.

"I had an incurable disease that was ruining my body. It had to be a digital brain for me. No other choice. But I guess if I could enjoy a healthy cyborg body I'd try it." Unexpectedly deep. Rick hadn't considered that choice wasn't always given. When nature deprives you of things, there is no point in arguing.

"My body was practically destroyed during the war. My brain was preserved, and when the technology was ready, I got this body." Everyone fell quiet again. Looks like Arthur hadn't told his friends he was a veteran of the war. This guy had some severe trauma. Rick wondered if other brain androids would be like that.

"Fuck. I'm so sorry to hear about your shit guys. Life's a bitch and…" Rick didn't finish his sentence because death was meaningless. It was all just transformation. Even if you really died apparently your soul was just recycled by the Universe.

"Don't worry about it and to answer your question. I would have loved being a badass cyborg like your friend Brock Dynamite." Everyone laughed. After that, the conversation went back to much lighter topics, mostly about all the times Brock had kicked ass. Rick took his leave from the group after regaling them with a few tales of mischief and Dynamite.

◆ ◆ ◆

Rick needed a walk. To Pigalle. It was about an hour walk but a pleasant one. The visit to the bar had been informative, and now it seemed obvious he'd have to follow the more difficult path before him. In the meantime, Rick would stroll to Pigalle. He ambled towards the Seine at a leisurely pace. He was crossing l'Alma bridge when a ship stopped to hover above him. A hatch opened, and a tractor beam shot down to capture Rick. In a moment they were gone. The craft shot up into the sky and disappeared among the stars.

Rick's current predicament landed him in a dark room. The light above the door just about illuminated what seemed to be cargo. *Cargo bay.*

"Mr Archer!" *I know that voice.*

"Dick Prunce?!" *Shit!*

"How good of you to join us!" Rick stood up and faced the entrance not knowing what to expect.

"Please come to the lounge. I've sent an orb to guide you." The door to the corridor opened and one of those PA orbs Amy hated appeared. Rick got up and followed the thing through the ship. This was a spaceship. An opulent craft. *Very nice.* He'd seen ads. *Starseeker 1138.* The space yacht could sleep twelve guests and twelve crew. Interstellar flight capability, fully panelled in mahogany, marble bathrooms and many more unnecessary luxuries. Rick was a little jealous.

The Dick was waiting in the lounge. Several scary looking Brock-sized cyborgs were also in the room. Rick immediately felt uncomfortable.

"Ah, Mr Archer welcome!" Dick's features darkened as he stood and gestured towards the sofa. "Rick, have a seat." Rick didn't. He just stood in the middle of the room, unmoving. "Sit down! Do it now and fucking open your ear holes." The tone let Rick know he should oblige. He took a seat on the left side on the massive u-shaped sofa, as far away as possible from the Dick. "Look, I thought we needed to talk a bit more. Make sure we see eye-to-eye. I want to make sure the show's next ten years are the best they can be. And I'm going to need your help. I can't do this without you." Dick had moved up next to Rick and put his arm around his shoulders. He could feel his strength. *Fucking cyber body.* "I need you to listen very carefully because the next part is critical." Dick squeezed Rick a bit more, it hurt. "See here's the deal. We're going to approve the Solus Tour series. It's going to be great for you to get off Terra. It's also going to be great for the colonies and making the Council look good. However, we don't want you getting any ideas while on your little adventures."

Dick squeezed Rick a little harder. It hurt a lot more. "Ideas like escaping or getting modifications. So we're going to delete the key to your digital brain. Which means that if you die there is no backup, you're dead." Dick paused for effect. It worked. Rick's unease was growing. "But that won't be a problem if you just come back. We can generate a new key by syncing your brain with your digital brain. Oh, and if you attempt to create another key from another brain copy, it will self-destruct." Dick released Rick from his death embrace and waited a moment for everything to sink in. Rick had nothing to say. Dick had more though. "We also wanted to warn you against stupid things like running away or trying to fake your death. The fine cyborg gentlemen assembled here today would hunt you down and destroy you. I wanted you to meet them." Rick looked around the room at the monsters that eyeballed him menacingly. "So stick to your contract and do your job and there will be no problem. You will not get a better offer, Mr Archer." Rick was drunk, so he had a bit of defiance left in him.

"But I can just kill myself?" The question clearly annoyed Dick.

"Mr Archer", Dick managed a calm voice and demeanour, "suicide voids the contract, and we'll delete your copy. But we will only terminate you if you break the contract. So as long as you do the show and stay human, you will have nothing to worry about. If you want to clear your bucket list you're going to have to play ball, you won't be able to stop for cocktails and museums if you're on the run." Rick's face hardened. His mind started racing, and he suddenly felt very hot. *Time to end this meeting.*

"Fine, I'll play ball. But I'm doing it for the people." Rick half-meant it, so he looked convincing enough saying it.

"Great, that's what I wanted to hear." Dick beamed a smile so big it had to be fake. "I see no reason to keep you any longer. Where shall we drop you off? Though I do recommend, you go home and get some rest."

"Just in Paris near where you found me." Rick felt his organs levitate as the ship dropped back down to Earth.

Amy was waiting for Rick near the bridge where they abducted him. He walked towards Amy with his usual nonchalance. He wasn't too fazed by the meeting, but he was pissed off. Something the Dick had said. The Agency was spying on him, they were on to him. But they couldn't know his plan. He didn't know his plan. For once his history of erratic behaviour would be an advantage. Amy was hovering in front of his face now, expectantly.

"Hey, Ames. How's it going?" Rick knew that would piss her off.

"Don't fuck with me? What happened? Who was that?"

"Who do you think? The Dick... He wanted a word in private."

"To say what? Come on Rick this is serious."

"To threaten me, and tell me escape attempts were futile. Amy these fuckers are fucking spying on me, and I think they're using Brock."

"Brock wouldn't betray you."

"Well, it sure fucking seems like he has. Dick mentioned my bucket list and used the same words Brock did. He tattled."

"Don't jump to conclusions, Rick. Dick Prunce is devious. There are many ways he could be spying on you. It could be through spy AIs, it could be through people following you, the psychiatrist, security systems, who knows? Don't just assume it's Brock. But we should find out, and you need to be more careful with what you say."

"Yes yes, you know me. I always follow my carefully laid out plans." He didn't.

SEASON FINALE

It was early. Too early to be at work. Rick was back in the 363. He didn't think he'd be returning to the tower, but the Universe loved messing with the living and their plans. It's one of the main reasons Rick objected to planning. Barry had organised a meeting with The Last Human team. Solus Tour was on the agenda. Then Rick had to get on with the season 10 final episode. He didn't even know what the last episode was about. First, he met Barry in his office. Brock was there, but Rick was wary of him. Rick hey-ed them and their AIs and went up to Barry's desk.

"Right, contracts to sign? Let's get on with it."

"Don't you want to read it first?" Barry handed the holo-doc to Rick.

"Amy, come here. I'm going to swipe through the pages, and you read them. Then tell me if there's fuckery I should worry about in there." Rick gave Barry a look that said: "happy now". He took a look at the document and started swiping while Amy scanned the pages. "So anything sneaky been added in there?"

"The contract includes the brain amendment you asked for and the Solus Tour provisions. I think you know what's in there." Rick knew. His late night talk with the Dick had been more than clear. Clearer than any contract could be. "Don't escape, do your job, don't get modifications, or they delete your digital brain. You do all that, you can live in an artificial body after you die and do as you please."

"No new and exciting sneakiness hidden in there?" Rick's eyes went from Amy to Barry a couple of times. "No?"

"I think DP knew we'd take a closer look at the contract this time around. So no funny business." Barry offered a smile, Rick smiled back.

"Amy, are you fucking sure I can sign this?"

"Yes go ahead." Rick started signing each page while swiping backwards. To sign he had to press his thumb in a box at the bottom of each page. It pissed him off.

"It's 2056, I can't believe I have to mark every fucking page."

"You don't. Just stay pressed in the square and it will auto sign all the pages." Rick was happy about this and showed his appreciation by not making any more comments, he just finished and handed the doc back to Barry. "Alright then, shall we get to the team meeting?"

"Lead the way." Rick followed Barry out, Brock grunted and followed Rick.

The meeting room was down on the studio floors. The Last Human Show had the entire 244th floor and half of the 245th. Higher ceilings in the studio bits. The show had its own editing and special effects facilities, meeting rooms, office space and the all-important catering services. Barry led them to meeting room two. The production team answered to Rick, but for the last decade, his only requests had been for more booze and drugs. These guys had had free reign for years, and the new hands-on Rick might come as a shock to them. Especially as he was created in the last few days and nobody in the room would know him yet.

A week ago Rick was his usual despondent self. Drunk or high or both. Maybe with a hooker in tow. Rick took his seat at the head of the oval table. That was new. Gary, the director usually sat there. Gary walked in first. He saw that Rick had taken his seat and couldn't hide his surprise. He sat next to Rick opposite Barry. Gary was a cyborg and apart from this gig he hadn't done much else. A few shorts and slasher movies. He had one of those annoyingly positive attitudes to life, upbeat about everything. It annoyed Rick, but he was usually too drunk to care. The producers and production managers followed closely behind. The money guy, the guests and locations guy and the marketing guy who worked directly with the Agency. A Dick Prunce stooge. Rick nodded to them. He had never bothered to learn their names. They were never really around. What was the point? Everybody took their seats, and Barry told them about Solus Tour. They liked it. Rick waited for Barry to finish and stood up to address everyone.

"This is big. We need to move away from the repetitive crap we've been peddling in recent years." Rick had been less than helpful and the main reason the show hadn't evolved. The irony was probably not lost on them. Rick didn't know much so they would still do their jobs as always. Now with more new and improved Rick. "I'm going to be a hands-on exec from now on. Let's make this show great again!" Rick faced the producers. He wasn't sure who did what so he addressed the lot. "I need a list of all the locations and people worth meeting from Luna to Eris. What else… Ah yes! We'll need the travel times between all the locations. How many days, weeks, months or years is it going to take to see all Solus has to offer?" Rick stopped and thought for a second. "Money. This is going to cost money. Make sure we don't run out." The one on the left nodded. The money guy. Then Dick's marketing stooge spoke.

"The show is also about showing how united we are and how the Council keeps us together. We want to show how well connected Terra, and the colonies are. The best way to do this is only using public transport. This will highlight the great infrastructure work of the Council and enable Rick to meet interesting people and keep costs down as a bonus." Everyone thought that was a great idea. Rick knew the motivation behind it though. The Dick didn't want Rick to have his own ship.

"This is genius, The Last Human travelling Solus on public transport! This practically sells itself! This is going to be huge! And the filming opportunities will be epic!" Gary was overjoyed. He was going on about equipment and guerrilla filming.

"OK guys. You have lots to talk about, plus you have this season finale to get done. I'll leave you to it." Barry gave them a wave and left. After a short while, everybody knew what they had to do, and the conversation shifted to the task at hand.

"We're doing Atlantis! It was the first episode, and a lot has changed since. We thought it'd be a nice anniversary thing. But now it's actually the last episode since we're moving on to Solus Tour. First episode and last episode! This is perfect! It's meant to be!" Gary was just having the best day. *Twat.* Rick didn't even remember that he'd been to Atlantis. He was continuously plastered throughout his thirties but still thought he'd have remembered something like Atlantis. He'd been dreaming about going for the last few months. Maybe during some meeting, he'd heard the team planning the episode over the sounds of his snoring. *Inception.* Rick was going to Atlantis for the first time, again...

"We'll take a look at how the city progressed over the years. The underwater expansion, the inclusion of dolphin citizens and all that Rick charm the fans love." The producers continued talking, but Rick's mind had stopped on the thing about dolphins. He'd read about the research when he was a kid, but now there was an actual city where people and dolphins cohabited. *Who wouldn't want to see that?*

"It's going to be great Rick! Not as great as Solus Tour, but an amazing way to end the show!" Gary had his hand up now. It would stay there until Rick did the deed. Rick high-fived Gary. "Awesome! Let's get this show on the road. The crew is probably done prepping the gear, our ship awaits." Rick smiled when he thought about his escape and how much it was going to bum Gary out.

❖ ❖ ❖

New Atlantis sat on the Atlantic Ocean off the Azores coast. It was nowhere near as big as the continent described by Plato, though like the continent of old, it too was sinking into the ocean. Except this time, it was voluntary.

The city had been expanding underwater to accommodate its new inhabitants. Gary was explaining this and more while he briefed Rick on the flight to Atlantis. Using solar, wind, tidal, and biomass, the artificial island-city fulfilled all its energy needs. Like Zero Cities, Atlantis was a self-sustaining ecological haven. The city was dominated by a great fin, a mile high and even deeper. The fin stabilised the artificial island against tsunamis and severe storms. It also served as an ocean cleanser. In combination with the outer barrier and security wall, it captured trash and funnelled it to the fin factory for recycling. Ocean waste was then re-purposed as building materials for maintaining the city and creating sustainable marine architecture and artificial reefs. Four Zero Cities surrounded the fin. Smaller domes and buildings dotted the island-city floor, winding roads lined with exotic trees connected everything. The architects had built artificial lagoons, hills and ridges to create a diverse landscape and environment for the Atlanteans.

Below the city floor, a mirror city existed in underwater spheres connected by a network of walkways and tunnels. Like an iceberg, there was more underneath than above. Rick saw some pictures of the upside-down city, it looked like the complex molecular structures that had baffled him since childhood. Each of these spherical modules was a self-contained, self-sustaining city. The submerged parts of the city were designed for use by dolphins and people. Dolphins used specially engineered hatches and moved from section to section via partly flooded tunnels. Rick was annoyed at being lectured by Gary during the whole flight but he was also excited.

The Last Human crew landed near the fin in front of what looked like an official building. They were greeted in fanfare by fans and some people probably in charge of something. The camera bots were rolling; they had been filming since they left the 363. Rick went to some fans and posed for pictures. He would play the part of good Rick, for now. Gary was talking to the Atlantean representatives and called Rick over. He finished up with his fans and gave them a catchphrase, they all laughed. They were still chanting when Rick reached Gary and the people in charge.

"Mr Archer it is a great honour to have you back in Atlantis. I am Siphon, one of the administrators here. We hope you enjoy your visit. And if there is anything we can do to help, please let us know." Siphon was an aquacyborg like many Atlanteans. Their upgrades enabled them to spend extended times submerged and swim fast enough to follow dolphins. The Atlantean upgrade package included underwater breathing and communication with optional sonar and echolocation. As Rick inspected Siphon, he realised that the Atlantean upgrade package was this week's episode's product push. *I want that.* And everyone else would want it too.

"Hi Siphon, call me Rick. This is Amy, my AI companion. We're excited to be here." Rick was trying to sound professional. Which was a lot easier when sober. Siphon did some sort of polite bow-nod and invited Rick and crew to follow him.

Rick started following while Gary gave instructions to the camera bots. Siphon explained he'd be taking them on a walking tour of Atlantis. It was all impressive enough, but very similar to any old Zero City, and Rick just wasn't that interested in the history and architectural wonders of Atlantis. He wanted to talk to some dolphins. Still, he listened and walked on and pretended to be interested. It took the better part of the morning to explore the city above ground. Rick felt his spirits lift when Siphon announced that they would be heading to the underwater portion. *After lunch...*

◆ ◆ ◆

The submerged city could be accessed from almost anywhere, but Rick was ill-equipped for most routes. Siphon led them to a dry hatch, and they descended through a glass tunnel into a semi-submerged walkway. Water filled about a third of the tube. They walked towards one of the main spheres. Through the glass, the mesmerising wonder of Atlantis captured Rick's full attention. If Siphon was talking Rick wasn't hearing it. Siphon was talking. He was explaining how all the city sections were connected.

Rick was finding it hard to move through the water and was beginning to fall behind. "Hey Siphon." Rick caught up with great difficulty and tapped the Atlantean on the shoulder, "I can't do this anymore. Walking through this water is hard." Gary was connected to the camera bots via neural link, but he still felt the need to gesture at them to get out of each other's shots. Rick scowled at Gary. That fuck always knew when he was about to go through something humiliating. Good TV was coming. "I don't have robot legs like you lot." Siphon had indeed forgotten all about Rick's lack of modifications, everybody always did. But they were in the middle of a submerged path so they'd have to continue anyway.

"Mr Archer, I'm so sorry. I should have considered your handicap earlier. We will use the dry paths as much as possible. May I suggest you swim in the meantime." *Handicap. Dick.* Rick shot daggers at Gary who could barely contain his mirth. Siphon made his statement so seriously, fans were going to love it.

Rick lowered himself in the water and starting swimming. The group continued with Rick swimming beside Siphon, the camera bots captured everything. Gary's chuckling probably included too. The tunnel ended in a pool at one of the sphere's many entrances. Siphon showed Rick the way out of the pool and back onto dry ground. The underwater city was similar to the above ground version except some areas were flooded and semi-submerged walkways connected them to other underwater sections. What truly blew Rick's mind were the floating blobs of water. The dolphins jumped to and from these blobs to access higher levels of the city. Each blob had a small spherical device in the centre, probably some sort of gravity device. He'd have to ask Amy later. These blobs enabled dolphins to navigate the city in ways suited to their physiology which was an absolute joy to behold. The acrobatic display mesmerised Rick.

Siphon was taking them to meet the dolphin administrator for Atlantis. From what Rick understood the dolphin administrator was the equivalent of Siphon, and he ran the city's underwater expansion and integration with the environment. Doctor Bubbles or Bubbles was a cyber-enhanced dolphin. This was becoming common among Atlantean dolphins. Living with aquacyborgs in cities made the dolphins realise that although they were perfectly equipped for life in the ocean, they had not the appendages necessary to build and manipulate objects and machinery. Once dolphins had their brain cyber-enhanced and the neural plate installed, they could start adding away. The most common upgrade was the neck arms. Also very popular among cyborgs. One or more telescopic arms plugged into the neural plate. Very useful for manipulating objects in front of your face or anything if you're a dolphin. Rick had always wanted those. *Who wouldn't want more arms?* Dolphins tended to also get the language and voicebox upgrades to converse in human speech; mostly because when cyborgs attempted to speak in clicks and whistles, it made dolphins laugh uncontrollably. So much so that it systematically killed conversations.

Siphon was explaining that as research in communication evolved it had become clear that dolphins already understood humans, but the human brain wasn't equipped to understand their speech. Creating trust had been the most significant barrier to two-way communication. Getting them to trust people and forgive them for their barbaric ways proved difficult. Eventually, dolphins had been convinced to communicate, though to this day whales had still not forgiven humans. Dolphins reach out to them every once in a while. Try to convince them that people on the surface have changed, that they're not really humans anymore. Even though dolphins and aquacyborgs have been actively restoring the oceans of the world for years and people have mostly stopped hunting and eating animals; whales had yet to be convinced. The trauma was severe.

◆ ◆ ◆

Bubbles' office was basically in a pool with holoscreens and projections on the walls above the water surface. He swam about and looked at stuff, did some things with his little arms and swam over to another screen before noticing the camera bot on the threshold. Gary had made everyone wait while he got some "raw Bubbles". Siphon and Bubbles exchanged a few meaningful glances and the aquacyborg took his leave.

"Ah, The Last Human!" Bubbles' voice was squeaky and robotic. Exactly the way Rick imagined a cyborg dolphin's voice would sound. He let out a whistle and laughed. "That was my name in dolphin, but you can call me Bubbles." And Bubbles laughed some more. Rick wanted to pet Bubbles and hug him, but he didn't think that would go down too well.

Normally at this point, the host would offer a seat, but there was no furniture in sight. Rick assumed one just had to stand there in waist deep water. He was wrong. A compartment opened up in the ceiling and floaties fell into the pool. "Please get comfortable." Rick grabbed an inflatable chair and tried to hoist himself up. He failed several times to get on. Each time captured on camera. Gary was pleased. Rick could tell from the incessant micro-celebrations. Once everyone had taken their seats and was gently bobbing on the water Bubbles started again. "I take it you enjoyed your tour of Atlantis so far." Gary immediately started listing the things he'd loved most about the city. Rick said he was impressed but found their world inconvenient for a lowly human.

"I mean this city is a marvel to behold. Really. This is like the stuff I saw in comics when I was a kid. I love it. But it's simply not for me. I can't swim too well, and I can't breathe underwater. So I can't really make the most of your fine city." Rick wished he had the Atlantean package and was sad that if he ever got it, he probably wouldn't be coming back anyway.

"Well, I have good news then. In anticipation of your arrival, we prepared an armoured nanosuit that would help you navigate our city and oceans. It is unique and our gift to you." Rick didn't know what to say, so he said thank you, always a good place to start. Bubbles looked up at the ceiling, and another compartment opened. All expected Rick's suit to fall out. Instead, a load of what seemed to be sex toys designed with dolphins in mind dropped down. "Don't pay attention to any of that. Wrong compartment." Bubbles laughed. Dolphins were well-known sexual deviants. Rick liked this Bubbles guy a lot. Another compartment opened and this time a suit fell out. It was bright yellow which made Gary laugh for some reason. "Mr Archer this suit was designed with you in mind. This power suit increases your strength and resistance. It will protect you against injury and temperature fluctuations. It is interwoven with a special nano-membrane that absorbs oxygen and enables you to breathe underwater without the need for cumbersome oxygen tanks. Among the other cool little gadgets, you'll find the nanosuit incorporates its own communications equipment, hydro-thrusters to help you swim faster and the visor has all the visual enhancements you could wish for. Best of all, you control it with brainwaves. Also, it's yellow so we can spot you from afar!" Bubbles laughed and then took a more sombre tone. "Unfortunately the suit can't make you understand or speak dolphin. Actually, I'm not sure that's a problem." Bubbles started laughing again. Everyone else joined in. Rick wasn't sure he got it, but he laughed anyway. He put the suit on and immediately felt amazing. He could feel the suit drying his body. He imagined this is what it felt like to be a cyborg. Rick wanted to test the suit out. "Do you like it, Mr Archer?"

"I fucking love it! Holy Universoul ballsack this is awesome! Thank you! Thank you so much!" Rick was looking over the suit excitedly. "You my friend, are a legend!" Bubbles laughed.

"I'm glad you like it. It's a gift."

"Thank you, this means a lot."

"Right! Now we can proceed with the tour. There is a fully submerged tunnel that starts at the bottom of the office. Follow me." And with that bubbles dove into the depth of his office and led the group through the tunnel.

Cyborg dolphins can project thoughts into people's minds, something to do with their brains. Cyborgs, however, require both parties to have the neural link upgrade to communicate via thought. This is not something dolphins advertised and they only used their ability when absolutely necessary. This was such a time. Rick was in the process of finding this out as Bubbles projected his thoughts into his mind. Without the suit, the signals would have been scrambled and just felt like a headache to Rick. But the suit enabled him to understand Bubbles as clearly as a conversation, clearer even.

"Rick this is Bubbles, I am speaking to you directly, in your mind. I just need you to listen, don't say anything." Bubbles waited an instant. Rick said nothing. *"Thank you. Rick, we need your help."* The plot thickens. He wasn't sure he could handle things getting more complicated. Bubbles explained there was a loose association between all the water cities of the world. Although aligned with the vision of Zero Cities and the Council, aquacyborgs and dolphins believed it was time for them the get representation on the Council. Bubbles wanted Rick to use his voice and the show to speed up the process. The Last Human Show coming to Atlantis was the long-awaited opportunity to get some recognition. *"Will you help us? I know you can't answer but if you just find a way to mention it today. That could be what it takes to elevate us and enshrine our rights."* All Rick could think about was he had no rights or representation, but he'd help anyway. Anything to mess with the Council and Agency.

The rest of the day was great. Rick swam, fast. Through tunnels and pools and the deep. He played with dolphins, and they showed him the kind of work they got up to. Which it turned out was anything people could do now that they could plug bionic arms in. The day wore on, and Bubbles had to get back to his duties. He dropped them off near a surface hatch. He and Rick shared a hug much to Rick's delight. It had taken a hilarious minute or so for Rick to figure out how to remove his gloves, but it had been worth it. He'd always wanted to feel dolphin skin. *So slick and soft.* He wasn't disappointed.

Siphon was waiting for them at the tunnel exit. "I hope you've enjoyed your time in Atlantis. It was an honour and pleasure to host you." They had, and for once it was Rick saying so excitedly.

"Siphon your city, and its people are wonderful. Aquacyborgs and dolphins have built something truly unique that clearly sets them apart from other species. The way of life of aquacyborgs is so different to land cyborgs. They're more different than robots and androids. And dolphins... Well dolphins, from what I can see, are people just like the rest of us. I've learnt so much today, thank you!" Siphon smiled and thanked Rick profusely. That would do. Rick had done his part.

Siphon led them back to their ship. Rick was following when his eyes stopped on the craziest vehicle he'd ever seen. A car-sized water tank with a dolphin inside using mechanical neck arms to steer. The car seemed powered by a watermill-looking engine. The dolphin's tail movements supplied the propellant. *Crazy dolphins.* Rick watched the dolphin drive away with a smile on his face. They were back at the ship just as night was falling. The whole city lit up, and Rick thought good things about Atlantis. Gary was talking to Siphon. Probably about important things to do with the show. The camera bots were wandering around capturing some more cutaways. Brock approached Rick. He'd been there all day following at a distance, not saying a word. *Does he know I'm pissed at his traitorous ass?*

"What do you want Brock? I'm not in any danger at the moment, or am I? If Brock didn't know before. Now he did. Rick was angry.

"We need to talk." *Ominous*, thought Rick.

"About what?" Brock started walking, and Rick followed

him. Their AIs stayed back.

"Where are you taking me? Has the Dick put a hit out on me or something? That was quick, never even made it to the Moon." Rick laughed nervously. *Had he?*

"The Agency has been spying on you." Brock had led Rick indoors into a loud bar.

"What are we doing here? Don't get me wrong I'd love a drink. But this is not you. What's going on in that big head of yours." Rick was heading to the bar. *When in Rome...*

"I needed to get away from the ship and crew. They're all potential spies for DP. Indoors and loud is safer from prying eyes and ears."

"I don't have any money. Amy pays for shit. Can you get this? Cheers."

"Rick this is serious." Brock paid for the drinks.

"What that the Agency is spying on me? Yeah, I figured that one out but thanks."

"OK, Mr Know-it-all. The Agency was using me to spy on you..."

"Duh!" Rick had felt the need to interject at this point to let Brock know that he knew what he was up to.

"Rick it's not like that so shut your face and listen." Brock made the accompanying "zip-it" hand gesture. "After the meeting at the Agency, I got suspicious. Some of the stuff Dick said... So after I dropped you off, I went to see an old buddy of mine. From pre-Rick days." Rick was still listening. "I asked him to give me the once-over, and something immediately popped up on the screen. Don't freak out." Rick perked up. *Why would I freak out?* "There was a flea-sized bot just sitting on my brain capturing data from my senses and relaying it to something bigger." Rick recoiled in disgust. He'd watched a documentary on brain hacking with insects microbots. Remote hacking was nigh on impossible these days. Had to get inside somehow. "You're not the one got hacked. So chill. My friend removed the fucker. He told me it'd been there for less than two days. You know what that means? The fucking shrink told on you." Rick was surprised for an instant. He thought doctor-patient privilege still meant something. Then Rick realised they probably hacked the doc and everyone else. Gary, the camera bots, fucking Barry. If they got Brock, they got everyone. "Look you don't need to worry about me. I've installed a defence mechanism. Anything tries to get in my face holes, it fries." Rick wanted that. He wondered if his brain was hackable. "They are willing to go to great lengths to keep tabs on you. I think you might be more important than you think." This is precisely what Rick wanted to hear. Which made him very suspicious. He couldn't really verify Brock's story.

"OK, Brock. Let's say you're telling the truth. Does this mean you're on my side? Even if it means death..."

"Yeah I'm with you, but I feel I should tell you; I have a copy tucked away in a secret location. The moment I die the other Brock activates with all my memories."

"Well aren't you the lucky cunt." Rick glowered.

"Hey if we're going off script I don't see why we can't hook you up along the way." Brock raised his glass and Rick met it.

"I'll drink to that!" They finished their drinks and headed back to the ship making a big show of having had a bunch of shots in celebration. Gary sent the camera bots to film them. Rick rushed towards the closest one and grabbed his camera head.

"See you all in two months for new adventures! In space! That's right the Last Human is going into space! Solus Tour coming soon!"

There would be hype. Rick knew it, there was no going back now.

MOM AND POPS

Rick had been on holiday since the season finale. He spent a lot of his downtime travelling Earth. He'd revisited Atlantis several times. During the summer aquacyborgs and dolphins of the world had created a united movement campaigning for their inclusion into the Council. The momentum afforded by Rick's intervention on The Last Human was not wasted. Support for their initiative was growing among Zero citizens. It seemed people were keen on getting dolphins involved in government. Bubbles would become Councillor, and he would win by a landslide. *Councillor Bubbles,* it made Rick chuckle every time he thought about it. The summer demonstrated Rick's influence over the masses. A power even he underestimated.

Rick had behaved during the break. Most importantly no drunken escape rants. He'd been doing a great job of promoting Solus Tour. The fans were excited. But it was bittersweet for Rick. He was glad to be leaving and excited about his new life, but he was a bit sad at leaving Earth behind. He'd be gone soon, maybe forever. Very few who left ever came back. Rick wondered, *was it the distances, were the colonies better?* He'd find out soon enough. In the meantime, he'd travelled the world mostly making the most of his suit in water cities. The fun was over though; Solus Tour was set to begin soon.

Brock had suggested Rick get additional upgrades for his precious suit and had taken him to one of his trusted friends.

The guy was huge just like Brock but much older. He had a long greying beard and stained overalls, he was rocking a black bandana with skulls and bones. Rick liked the style. Cyborg-bodybuilding-wizard-mechanic. Strong look. It turned out this guy had been handling Brock's upgrades since day one. Pops, it's what everyone called him, had found young feral Brock and fixed him, raised him and trained him.

Pops' workshop was nestled between Robot Town and the great towers of 6-6, a place called Boxtown. This area had been added when independent cyber surgeons made the case that the towers were not an adequate place of business for their trade. They required dark alleys and catered to shifty individuals, something in between the Pit and Robot Town. They won their case, and Boxtown was built. Units stack on top of each other and next to each other to create a confusing maze. Looked a lot like a cargo yard. Boxtown was renowned for its cheap cyber-enhancement workshops and temp mutation labs. This was where party animals and people who wanted to stay off grid came for their upgrades. Pops' workshop was somewhere in the middle of this maze. Rick would never find his way out if Brock left him there.

To Rick, the workshop looked like an indoor junkyard, but apparently, all these components were useful and some rare, supposedly.

"So this is the famous Rick. He's smaller than he looks on TV." *Good start* thought Rick.

"Yeah, they always film it, so I look taller. TV magic eh!" *Nothing, OK.* "Thanks for taking a look at my suit. Brock says you're the best." Rick tried a smile.

"And you believe him? Brock is a fool! Wasting his life on the likes of you!" *Ah, so there it is.* Rick didn't really know where to go from there.

"That's enough Pops! We all make our own decisions, he's made his, and I've made mine. Now can you just improve this suit? I know you'll know what to do." Brock dropped the suit on a workbench and turned to Rick. "Let's go. He'll do a great job;

you'll be better than Iron Man!" Pops shook his head and muttered under his breath while they walked away laughing. "So Rick, do you think you'll be able to survive without the suit?" Brock laughed. Rick didn't think it was so funny. He'd grown accustomed to the suit. Without it, he felt weak and insignificant again. When he'd gotten back from Atlantis, he'd refused to take it off for a week straight, sleeping in it even. It destroyed his mattress. They'd eventually pried him out to clean the suit and wash him.

"I'll get by. Probably just hide out at home. I know Mom will be pleased I don't have the suit on." They both chuckled.

Rick had destroyed a few parts of the house because of miscalculated strength. But he didn't care. The suit had an empowering effect, though he'd also damaged a few cabs, his Uber rating was down to three. Brock ordered them now. They got back to Rick's and headed to the kitchen for a bite. Rick had been eating and drinking at home more lately. His celebrity had reached extreme levels after Atlantis. It'd become difficult for him to be in public.

Rick had Gousto prepare a couple of fancy burgers and they munched away in silence, until Mom spoke. "Rick where's your power suit? I didn't see you walk in with it?" Mom clearly enjoyed saying that.

"It's getting upgrades. Don't worry I'll have it back in no time." Mom didn't reply. Rick took another bite out of his burger and turned to Brock who'd already demolished his burger. There was nothing left. It almost seemed like the plate had been licked clean.

"So Rick... What's the plan? We haven't really discussed the actual escape part of Solus Tour." Rick didn't really have a concrete plan. That's why he hadn't discussed it with anyone, and that's why he wasn't arousing suspicions. Rick was going to wing it, something cyborgs, robots and logical beings hated. Brock wouldn't like it.

"I think it's probably best we just do each section one at a time. Thinking too far ahead leads to disappointment when things don't work out." He grinned. Brock hated it when he was mysterious and philosophical.

"What escape?" Mom had joined in. Although she was aware of Solus Tour, she'd always assumed Rick would return. She was an AI, but AIs had feelings too. "When are you coming back from this Solus Tour?" Rick and Brock were still shooting blanks.

"Ummm…" That's all Rick could muster. Brock did no better.

"Mom let me sync with you." Once Amy synced with the house it would know everything Amy knew. She would probably be angry. The sync took a few moments, Amy hovered in front of one of the house ports and data was shared. Rick knew it was over when Mom started shouting. She was upset.

"I'm coming with you. I'm not staying in this empty house. My purpose is to keep Rick safe and healthy when indoors I will keep doing that. I can be the ship's AI."

"We're not taking a ship. The production is making us travel on public systems. They don't trust Rick."

"Rightly so!" Mom's synthetic voice betrayed sadness. It was unmistakable. "He's a sneaky liar."

"I was just trying to postpone this conversation because I didn't know what to say and I don't know what to do. I just have a final destination. But I'm not sure how I'm getting there."

"What's the destination?" Brock asked.

"Can't say." Rick was not telling.

"Can't say, or won't say?"

"Whichever you prefer." Rick wasn't telling, and that was that. But the subject was quickly brought back to Mom.

"So you were just going to leave me here and say nothing."

"I was going to call and stay in touch." He wasn't. In reality, Rick expected to be dead before episode three started shooting. But he couldn't tell them that. Mom and Amy would lose their minds.

"We could attach her to your suit's programming." Brock

burst out laughing. Amy's suggestion would work, apparently, but to have Massively Overbearing Machine in his head whenever he wore the suit would be intense for Rick, perhaps too intense.

"Yes! I love it, it's the best way to keep you safe!" *Fuck.* Rick couldn't believe this was actually going to happen.

"Calm down. Amy is there any other way? With you maybe?"

"No sorry Rick. Only one AI per cube and they don't sell blank cubes." Rick let out a long sigh. The giving up sigh.

"OK. Let's be clear. This is only a temp solution Mom. You're not living in my suit permanently. It will drive me crazy." Rick might have to wear the suit less, *never going to happen,* or find a ship or body for Mom.

"Yes I understand, only until you find me a ship or body."

"OK then." Rick started thinking about all those great times swimming in the ocean, enjoying his suit-given abilities, deep in thought, merging with the ocean. Then he added Mom's running commentary. *Fuck.*

IRON RICK

A few hours had passed, Rick had gotten away from Mom for one of the last times, and it was time for the Solus Tour team to attend their medical examinations. Going into space was not a mundane activity, especially not for a human.

Things were straightforward enough for cyborgs. They were handed a list of recommended augmentations to improve their comfort and survival chances when experiencing the rigours of space. These included a retractable inbuilt helmet and expanding nanomachine spacewalk units, as well as the all-important pressure adaptors and radioactive scrubbers. The robots were merely checked over to ensure they had no malfunctions brewing. They were already space-proof.

For Rick things were more complicated. As the good doctor was explaining; Rick was a human and no human had been into space for decades.

Most doctors in the world were great at upgrading and fixing bodies but preserving a frail body seemed pointless. But like Rick, they would need to fight the urge to upgrade.

"You see Mr Archer space and foreign worlds can be very traitorous, and if I understand, correctly you will be visiting every colony in Solus. That is…" The doc paused, *probably for effect,* "a wide variety of environments, some quite stressful for the body and mind." *Not a very good drop.* Rick was getting schooled on the dangers of space for a human. The cameras were rolling. *Episode 1: Rick is too shit for space what are we going to do about it?* The doc continued, "you see the moment you leave the safety of Terra everything becomes a hazard. Firstly, you can't survive the vacuum of space. Even your cyborg colleagues will need upgrades. Secondly, radiation permeates the Universe, and outside of shielded zones, it will destroy your cells. Stay in the ship and when the ship lands stay indoors or in the safe zones."

"Stay indoors. Check." The doc frowned.

"This is no laughing matter, Mr Archer. This trip will be the death of you if you do not take the appropriate safety precautions." Rick stopped smiling. He was tempted to say he was OK with dying but stopped himself. "The varying gravities and weightlessness will cause motion sickness, nausea and just general malaise, I've cleared a subcutaneous implant that delivers a drug for that. Another problem you'll encounter will be bone and muscle deterioration. Though the ships and planets will have artificial gravity that usually closely matches Terra this won't be at all times. Mr Archer our records show that you will most likely become the first human to spend such extended periods in space. And, well, we're simply not sure about the long-term effects on humans. There have been no studies. But we are practically certain the loss of bone and muscle mass will occur. So you will need to undergo muscle stimulation therapy daily."

"And what might that be?" It sounded unpleasant.

"We've created a chamber that will stimulate muscle and bone growth while you sleep."

"What so no bed?"

"Only when in transit Mr Archer. This will be better for your health. The chamber will also help stop fluid redistribution and minimise the psychological effects of space travel like poor sleep, high stress, enclosed spaces and homesickness." Rick didn't like the idea of being locked in some coffin while they travelled. He wanted to be awake when he died. "We think your extended travels will be easier and mostly painless if you travel inside the pod. Should the ship you are aboard be destroyed the pod is protected by additional shielding and possesses an engine and pilot AI to take you the nearest Council presence."

"What about the show? I'm supposed to be shooting a show about how easy it is to travel the stars in this wonderfully connected civilisation. How do I do it from the box?"

"I have been told you would do the scenes and adjourn to your pod."

"Fuck that!" Rick was having none of it.

"Mr Archer your safety is our main concern."

"Yes, I've heard that shit before." Rick turned to Amy all smug-like, "won't you send the good doctor the schematics to my suit." Still wearing his smug smile Rick turned back. "Doc I want you to tell me what modifications this suit needs to survive the perils of space," Rick said the last bit like he was narrating an old B-movie. The doc didn't say anything. The blank stare notified Rick that the doc was examining the suit.

"This is an impressive piece of technology. Who made this for you?"

"It's a gift from the Atlanteans."

"They have done excellent work. We hadn't even thought of a power suit. There's been no research in this field since the war as cyborgs have no need for them. But this suit can easily be modified to survive space. We will send the recommendations to your AI." Rick was pumped. *One epic space suit coming right up.* He was practically sure the Dick would be furious. *Bonus points.* Having Rick locked up in a coffin was probably his idea. *Not this time.* "Mr Archer. There is something else I wanted to discuss with you." The doc's voice had become more sombre. The kind of tone that precedes terrible news.

"What it is it?" Rick hesitantly asked the question.

"Your brain is deteriorating. Most likely a pre-existing condition exacerbated by the excesses of your lifestyle. This is easy to address but not without breaching your contract. The other alternative is healthier life choices. If you do not address this issue, your brain may become too damaged to be accurately scanned and cyberised." Rick was in shock. His brain was fucked. *Fuck.* He needed that digital brain encryption key or cyber enhancements or both. *Fuck.*

"What can you do doc?" Rick wasn't hopeful, but it was worth a try. The doc thought or flicked through his files. His eyes blinked a lot, and he was quiet for a minute.

"I will add medical provisions to my suit upgrade recommendations. The suit will administer medication and brain therapy. But Mr Archer this is not a cure. It will only delay the inevitable." Rick needed a hug. He wished Amy had arms, he considered Brock for a hug and then thought better of it. "I will have my recommendations over in the hour. I'm sorry I couldn't give better news Mr Archer. Good luck." Rick mumbled his goodbyes and left. Brock was in the waiting room.

"That took long enough. Are you cleared for space?" Brock seemed happy. Which was weird but Rick didn't care.

"He needs to upgrade his suit, and he'll be good to go!" Amy answered in her usual chirpy tone, and Rick was despondent.

"What happened in there Amy? Rick?" Brock said their names a few more times in case there was a magic number that would make them open their mouths. Amy broke first, her number was five.

"Rick has a brain problem, and he can't get the treatment as it includes modifications."

"Fuck, I'm sorry brother." Brock put his massive hand on Rick's shrinking shoulders.

"But it won't affect him for a while. So no need to commiserate, let's get going! Clock is ticking. Tic-Toc!" Amy started towards the exit.

◆ ◆ ◆

They had a big meeting at the 363. Solus Tour was about to take off. Rick was shaken, Brock dragged him and they followed Amy out the clinic. It was a short ride to the tower but long enough for Rick to come to his senses. The news about his brain meant he only had one real option left. He had to run and get cyber enhancements. His brain would never survive his life, and his digital mind would be destroyed by the Dick. Rick was going rogue. If there was any doubt before, it was gone now. In the interest of self-preservation, he would take massive life-threatening risks... The next thing to determine would be when to actually escape. Maybe finding out about the shooting schedule would help. Rick had given instructions and preferences and was looking forward to seeing what they'd planned for him.

Today they were using the big meeting room. The whole team was here. Not that it mattered to Rick who had no idea who anyone was. There were dozens of people in the room but as far as he knew Rick was only travelling with Gary and a few camera bots. *So who the fuck are all these people?*

Rick was about to find out that coordinating a reality documentary show shot in space and aired weekly was no simple task. Directed by Gary, the camera bots would shoot almost continuously. Footage would be viewed and roughly organised and sent to a relay production ship that would then beam the files back to Terra for editing and more of that TV magic before airing. Rick didn't like that. They could manipulate his words. They'd done it in the past. But there was nothing he could do about it for now. Gary was talking, and Rick thought he should listen a bit.

"We are almost set and ready to roll. From what I understand Rick needs a few adjustments to his now iconic suit, and he is set for space." Annoyingly everyone clapped at that. Someone shouted "Space Rick", and that made him smile. *Fuck yeah space Rick.* Gary wasn't done. He wanted to go through the whole season one episode plan. He was giddy like a schoolgirl. "Right later this week we're picking up promo shots, and then next week we are off. Episode one will be a mix of today's footage at the clinic and this meeting and... wait for it... our departure from Terra!" Everyone clapped again. Someone shouted "Solus Tour", and Rick wondered if it was the same guy. "Next week we meet here and travel to the Pacific, where we'll take the Japanese space lift to the Eastern Space Station where we'll grab the Moon shuttle." Gary paused. Rick had a question.

"Why? Couldn't we take off from this tower and just go to the Moon?"

"Yes, if we took an Uber Space. The Japanese space lift is the tallest tower in the world and the cheapest way to space." Rick found that hard to believe.

"You are doing this on a shoestring to show people how easy and cheap it is to travel." The Agency stooge had answered Rick before Gary could, but he would have said something similar, just probably more enthusiastically. Gary continued outlining the season episode by episode. Rick was listening but imagining his escape at each stage of the show. As Gary moved forward with the season's description, Rick realised there probably wouldn't be a show anymore by that point. He stopped listening and zoned out. It was all so far away. Everything would be different.

The meeting ended, and people shook hands, congratulated themselves and patted themselves on the back. Rick was the first out. None of that crap for him. He and Brock had to get back to Pops and check on the suit. Before he could leave The Last Human Studios, he was stopped by a familiar voice.

"Rick! Good to see you!" Rick froze. *The Dick.* He hadn't seen Dick Prunce since the abduction, not nearly long enough. "The Solus Tour has come together nicely! Good work! I look forward to catching the first episode." Rick composed himself.

"Dick! Good to see you!" Rick walked towards the Dick and extended his hand. The ensuing handshake almost broke Rick's hand and lasted an uncomfortable amount of time. "Didn't see you in the meeting there. Yeah exciting stuff! Can't believe it's all happening." Rick was keeping it together, wincing through the pain of the ongoing handshake. The Dick leaned in, real close to Rick's face.

"Don't make me regret this. Do not fuck up." With that the Dick released Rick. "Good luck!" The Dick walked away congratulating any and all he crossed paths with.

"That cunt!" Rick held his hand. The pain would pass. The anger would take longer. "If I had my suit I'd have kicked his face in." Brock put his hand on Rick's shoulder.

"Leave it. Let's get out of here." Rick followed Brock, and they got a taxi back to Pops' workshop.

Amy had forwarded the doctor's recommendations to Pops as soon as she'd gotten them. Night had come by the time they reached Boxtown. It looked even more pit-like in the dark. As it should. Boxtown was a common stop on the way to the pits. Needed a quick penis upgrade, a second butthole or maybe a sex tentacle? The neon glow of the sex workshops attracted all kinds of people on their way to play. Rick followed Brock through the maze enchanted by all the bizarre people on their way to become weirder for the night. Many of them would be back in the morning to normalise themselves before heading home. *What a great time to be a sex weirdo.* Pops had been busy all day making modifications to the suit. The duo walked into the workshop with their AIs close behind. Pops barely acknowledged them.

"I've been working on this suit of yours all day. Impressive craftsmanship. Those dolphins know what they're doing. I personally would've interwoven the suit with nanomachines so it would retract in and out of your boots and belt or something. But this is still outstanding work." Pops hadn't looked up. Still tinkering. "Oh and I received your doctor's requests, just finishing up."

"Can the suit support an AI?" Rick groaned when he heard the question. He'd forgotten about that. Amy forgets nothing.

"Yes, it currently has a simple AI assistant." Pops seemed annoyed at the question. "Right, so the suit will now protect Rick from the vacuum of space and scrub radiation. It has integrated bio-regenerative life support systems and medical treatment functions. The filtration systems have been modified to work in space. They will continue to filter toxins and absorb oxygen when possible. I've added air storage for three hours. Also, the suit will stimulate the growth of bone and muscle tissue to combat space atrophy."

"Will it hurt?"

"The fact that you ask this question tells me you are a little girl. So yes it will probably hurt." Brock started laughing.

"I pity the sissy!" Mr T added a little extra to keep Brock going. Pops was not laughing though.

"I've added a micro-engine with booster rockets..."

"You what? I can fly in the suit now?" Rick's eyes were wide, really wide, cartoon child wide.

"Yes. When in space. It won't lift you if there's gravity." Rick couldn't understand why Pops was acting like this wasn't the greatest thing ever.

"I've improved the armour, and added shock absorption, you can take a decent beating now. From someone like Brock even. But you'd still take a beating. Try not to get shot. Most projectiles will pierce the armour." Rick thought not getting shot was sound advice but resisted making any jokes. "I've boosted combat abilities a little, but any more and the suit would tear your muscles apart. You also now have plasma cannons built-in to each wrist and the targeting system is linked to your new and improved HUD and opticals. I've designed this so that any idiot child who's played video games can use this armour. Hopefully, you can manage." Rick couldn't think of any time in his life where he'd been more excited about something. He would be like Iron Man, but better. Pops stopped and finally looked up at Rick. His face had darkened somewhat. Different from the scrunched-up frown-face Rick had become accustomed to. "I'm just finishing the brain treatment system." Rick shrugged. He didn't care about that right now. Iron Rick was on his mind.

"This is great work Pops. I appreciate it, thanks!" Brock gave Pops one of those slow respectful triple nods, like you're hearing a good beat.

"Yes! Thank you so much, Pops! This is amazing! I can't wait to try it on." Pops' face returned to its angry frown.

"The suit's an eyesore. You need a paint job. This bright

yellow is ridiculous." The yellow was intense.

"What were you thinking?"

"I don't know it's your suit." Pops shrugged and turned away from the conversation.

"Brock?"

"I don't care."

"You're both so helpful aren't you? Weren't you super fucking soldiers back in the day?" Brock sighed.

"OK well, my first thought is you don't want to be seen so much anymore, do you?" Brock looked over to Pops. "You have some active camo paint?"

"If he's wearing the suit on TV I doubt they'll want him to shimmer and disappear with shifting lights."

"Good point." Brock had no more suggestions.

"Just paint it something less offensive to the senses." Rick thought about it and promoting the show on the suit would be a great way to avoid further suspicions.

"OK let's paint it black but keep some yellow stripes here and there. I'd like a big Solus Tour logo on the chest and The Last Human logo on the back." Pops seemed OK with that, and he went to hang the suit in a design and paint booth. He inputted Rick's preferences into the side panel, grunted and mumbled something disparaging when he saw the logos. Robot arms dropped down and started applying the designs. In a few minutes Rick's suit was ready, and it was glorious. He considered hugging Pops for an instant. He thought about how that would work out, at best he'd get floored. *Bad idea.* He'd just have to rejoice on his lonesome.

Brock was lying on the workbench, he turned his head to get a look at the suit and nodded in approval. Pops had begun tinkering on him. "Rick it's gonna take Pops a few hours to get all my upgrades done. Not sure you want to hang around."

"I wanna watch."

Pops' furrows deepened. "Don't get in my way." Rick wouldn't. He'd stay at a safe distance.

Rick was hoping the two of them would reminisce and

he'd discover a bit more about Brock's youth. They didn't. He learnt nothing. Pops just went through Brock's list of modifications and upgraded him. It took close to six hours; four hours longer than Rick had expected. After the first hour, Rick had put his suit on. He'd missed wearing it. *Never taking it off again.*

SOLUS TOUR

Rick felt like his guts were tied into a knot. Today was departure day. It's what he'd been waiting for, and it's what he desired more than anything. He was scared shitless nonetheless. Brock had arrived bright and early, and they'd sat together for breakfast. Rick would have liked a quiet meal, but that was impossible with Mom going on and on about how excited she was to be coming. Brock spent most of breakfast suppressing laughter while Rick just shook his head and ate his pancakes.

It was time to go. Amy had come in blaring it for the third and final time. Rick got his armoured suit on, that's all he was taking. He did consider taking his pillow for a second. It was so plump and soft. Rick often joked that with that pillow he'd find any rock comfortable. He imagined himself showing up in full armour with a pillow under his arm. *Maybe not.* He took a last walk around the house. He'd lived in this house for ten years. There had been many good times, but they were a long time ago, Rick was ready to get out of dodge. He went back downstairs, everyone was waiting. Rick walked up to one of the house's interface panels and placed his hand on it. It lit up, and Mom started downloading to the suit. In a few instants, she'd taken over for the AI assistant.

"I like it here. It's a bit tight, but the suit's programming is beautiful." And so it begins. Rick didn't know how long he would be able to handle this.

"OK let's go! The cab's outside." Amy hovered towards the door and waited for everyone to get out before locking up the house and activating the security system.

The flight to 363 was short, but it felt like an eternity to Rick. Mom was excited to be on the move for the first time. She saw the world through the suit's optical systems, and it was blowing her digital mind. Mom had been the house AI for ten years, and in that time she had seen inside and outside of their home. She had internet access, but this was different.

"Aaaah! Stop it!" Rick couldn't hold it in. The cab ground to a halt.

"What the fuck Rick?" Brock had switched to defensive mode. Amy and Mr T were scanning the environment.

"Are you alright sir?" Neither the taxi AI nor the others could hear Mom prattling on about the scenery. Rick realised this now.

"It's fine sorry. I was talking to Mom. You can resume the drive. Sorry." Rick had to figure out how to speak inside the helmet only. In the meantime, he just placed it on the dash so Mom could still see the scenery.

The Uber dropped them off at The Last Human Studio's loading dock on the 244th. The team was assembled and ready for the departure. Gary was there with his three camera bots. The rest would either follow in the production ship or stay behind. Rick walked up to Gary who, no surprise there, was very excited. The camera bots were in position and filming had begun. Barry had come to see Rick and Brock off. Rick felt a pang of sadness. He'd probably never see Barry again. He felt bad they hadn't told Barry about their plan. But they couldn't. It would have jeopardised everything. Rick gave a heartfelt hug to Barry. It felt different. A true hug. Rick's first goodbye forever hug.

"What schmoe? You going to miss me?" Barry started laughing. "I'll miss you too! But you'll be back in a few years and we can vid call anytime! You can tell me all about those space whores and fine drinking holes." Rick laughed, Brock laughed, Barry laughed, they hugged, it was great TV.

Gary signalled that it was time to go and they boarded the studio's ship. They were about to take off, and the Agency stooge appeared, boarded and took a seat.

"Sorry to keep everyone waiting." Rick had not realised that chinless prick was coming. Maybe he'd have to learn his name now. It was Dave, *what an absolute twat*. Rick started thinking about the complications this might create.

"Everybody on board, everybody ready?" Gary looked around and turned back to face the console. "Alright take us out." Everybody was waving, shouting and clapping. Rick wondered why they were all so pleased to be staying behind and doing their regular jobs. Then it hit him. They were happy and liked their jobs.

Japan had stayed the same mixture of ancestral architecture and futuristic technology as pre-war. Zero City 11 covered much of Japan now, but its shape had been adapted to the country's volcanic terrain and to preserve as much of the classic architecture as possible. No neon-lit streets or ancient temples for Rick this time around. They were headed south-east of the country. Far outside of city limits.

A disappointed Rick was just learning the Japanese Space Elevator was nowhere near Japan. It was actually in the Pacific somewhere on the Equator. It was the only way to maintain an anchor structure on the planet and a geostationary base in orbit. And building it in the ocean rather than land was deemed safer in case its hundreds of miles of cables were ever severed.

The lift was the cheapest way of getting cargo and people into space, costing barely more than a transatlantic cab ride. Even people living on UBI could afford a trip into space once in a while.

Unfortunately for the company that built it, the breakthroughs in inertial force and artificial gravity significantly improved space-faring vehicles rendering the elevator useless from day one. Before it was even operational, great factories were churning out perfectly safe vehicles that could leave and re-enter earth's atmosphere like it was nothing.

They'd built it, so they used it. And, because it was self-maintaining and repairing, it had been kept operational. Over time it had become a bit more of a tourist attraction though it did still transport large volumes of cargo.

Rick's gaze fell upon the giant artificial island. The structure was composed of a ground base protruding from the ocean, landing pads and a central terminal from which people boarded the large robotic cars. The cars travelled up a central rail made of smart nanocomposite materials and carbon nanotube tethers that adapted to changing atmospheric conditions. The entire thing was managed by an AI.

◆ ◆ ◆

The Solus team landed on one of the pads dotting the ground base. The camera bots rushed out and got into position to film Rick getting off the ship. One of the bots followed them as they walked in the terminal, one got a close up of the terminal sign, and the other got some cutaways of people going about their business, some landscape shots and few ships. It was going to be like this the whole time. Rick was starting to regret not taking the pod option. With Mom in his head, Dave the Agency stooge and those camera ninjas following him around things could get annoying quickly. *This is going to be long.* The terminal was not packed, and they did not queue for anything, they just walked straight through and into the cars. They found some seats by the windows. There were supposedly four passenger cars and four cargo cars. Though more often than not passenger cars carried cargo as well. Each car straddled one side of the x-shaped rails.

The cars were divided into levels, but passengers sat on the top level. It's the only one that offered a view of the space station on arrival. The cars were lined with floor to ceiling windows to give the best possible sights. They were about half full when the AI conductor announced the imminent departure. There were seats, but the ride was smooth, passengers were not required to sit if they didn't want to. Rick was not sitting. He was stood by the window looking out, giant clamps were slowly retracting. Gary walked up behind Rick.

"Right Rick. Let's talk to some of these passengers and find out where they're travelling to and maybe why if it's interesting!" All Rick could think was *for fuck's sake Gary!* But he'd play ball.

"That's a great idea but I think you should find out their stories first so we don't waste any time. Then bring the good ones to me here. We can use this amazing backdrop." Gary didn't argue but Rick could tell he didn't like it. Good, *now fuck off for a bit.*

Gary directed his camera bots, and they started exploring the passenger car for TV-worthy stories. Rick's attention returned to the departure preparations, the clamps were practically off, and machinery was coming to life. Suddenly the scenery was moving. The departure was smooth; not even the smallest of jolts as their ascent to the heavens began. Rick removed his helmet again; Mom's excitement was too much. He had to admit it was quite the sight, he too was in awe. Then he was annoyed. Gary was back to interrupt Rick's window gazing.

"Rick, meet Pete, he's a transporter." Gary pushed Pete closer to Rick. "Tell him what you're transporting, go on." Pete seemed a bit uncomfortable. He didn't want to be there. *That makes two of us mate.*

"Mr Archer..." Pete paused nervous-like, "I'm a big fan of yours." Pete was a big, tough-looking cyborg. His nervousness seemed out of place. Cool Rick would help him out.

"Pete", Rick dragged out the first e, "Chill my man, look at this epic view!" Pete approached, and Rick put his arm around as much of the cyborg as he could. "Now, how about you tell me about what you're transporting?" They had exited the troposphere and were passing the stratosphere. The awe-inspiring view was undeniably relaxing. Pete approached, and Rick shook his hand. "So Pete, my man, what are you so worried about?"

"I've never been on TV... And I'm not sure I should be

talking about the job."

"Is it confidential? Or military? Because unless you're a soldier, your cargo can't be that important." Rick laughed. Pete seemed to think about it for an instant.

"I guess you're right. It's not that important."

"And what might your destination be?" Rick was still intrigued.

"I'm heading to Proxima." It was said so casually though it was everything but for Rick.

"Wow! Amazeballs! Didn't expect this!" Rick tried to compose himself. "Right, so, this is exciting. OK, OK. So, why are you heading out of Solus?

"I'm transporting cargo to a theme park."

"Come on Pete, don't make me beg. Tell us what you're transporting. Everyone wants to know." Pete seemed to hesitate for a bit. Rick had to press him a little more before he broke. A bit of fake crying eventually did it.

"I'm transporting dinosaur embryos…" That was too much for Rick. He instantly reverted to age twelve, bouncing up and down and shouting "ooh" like a teen on a school bus watching a yo mama fight.

"Holy fuckballs that's fucking amazing!" Rick had to compose himself again. He kept shaking his head in disbelief at the camera. "OK, OK, so you're transporting dinos out to the Proxima colonies. Why? I think our viewers are going to want to know why."

"Sorry I'm just the transporter, but I'm guessing for rides or a petting zoo…. I just need to get these safely to their destination. Or I don't get paid." Rick wanted to go to that theme park. Twelve Jurassic Park movies had ensured no such park would ever grace the surface of Earth.

Rick grabbed one of the camera bots and asked the viewers how they thought the dinos would be used. He announced a poll and prizes for the winners. Dinosaurs had fascinated people of all ages since their discovery, and Rick was no exception. As a kid, he was really into this Ancient Aliens show. They had alternate history theories that involved aliens and although considered pseudoscience for a long time, in the end, they were somewhat vindicated. Although not entirely correct their interpretations were a hell of a lot closer to reality than religion ever got and even beat past century mainstream science in some cases. Rick thought back on the first post-war episodes.

The war had unearthed new fossils that showed humanity some incredible things. People literally didn't believe it. Rick did. He'd always wanted stuff like alien gods and dino-riding people to be real. And it's easier to believe when you want to. The truth was fossils rarely formed. Many species never fossilised. Unless something died in watery mud, there were no records of it. *Die anywhere else, and you're food.*

As Rick was often reminded, humans knew far less than they thought. Throughout history, greed and arrogance had interfered with their understanding of the world. The adventurers and scientist of old had lied to make themselves look good, and religion always stood in the way of results that damaged its dogma.

The discovery of irrefutable evidence of advanced civilisations dating back a hundred million years shocked humanity into humility. Artefacts and fossils pointed to the existence of dinosaur riding humanoids with advanced tools and nuclear power. *Fuck yeah.* Much to Rick's delight, these discoveries led the scientific community to start bringing extinct species back from nothingness. By then research had shown that most dinosaurs including the T-Rex were slow and no real threat to transhumans.

Though scientist could bring back these harmless giants, no parks had ever opened on Earth. The Jurassic Park law forbade it. It was a stupid law that may have made sense twenty years ago, but now the world was populated by superhumans. The threat was negligible. Rick had dreamt of riding a T-Rex for as long as he could remember. He might have to go to Pete's theme park...

Rick and Pete came off the dino tangent as the space lift

passed the Kármán Line. Gary was back with a girl and a dog. The girl was stunning. Just over shoulder length black and purple-bluish hair, green eyes, dressed in mostly black with a bright red T-shirt with a devil on the chest asking people if they felt lucky. She looked like a bit of a badass. The dog looked like a shepherd dog cross — good looking dog.

During his childhood Rick had played with and fed many stray dogs displaced by the war and purge. He loved dogs, but his lifestyle hadn't been very pet-friendly. Still, he had the gift with animals. Rick thanked Pete for his appearance while not-so-subtly pushing him away. The girl approached Rick seemingly against her will. Gary was still trying to convince her. *Sure knows how to pick them.* When they were close enough, Gary gave her a nudge into frame.

"Hi there! How might you be doing on this fine ascent?" Rick was trying to be charming, but it wasn't working. No answer came. *OK different tactic.* "And what might this little fella's name be?" Rick was down on one knee petting the dog now, giving it all his attention. The dog immediately took a liking to Rick, and the licking began. Rick was laughing trying to avoid the dog's lightning quick tongue as it lashed out at him. The girl smiled.

"This is Moondog, Moon for short. They call me Moongirl, also Moon for short." Rick wanted to ask her why but he held his tongue. He stood back up and extended one of his hands while leaving the other down for Moondog to lick. Moongirl shook his hand and smiled. Before Rick could follow up with his next questions, she spoke again. "So what's the Last Human doing on his way into space?"

"Have you not seen the adverts?" From her expression, Rick could tell she hadn't. "We're doing The Last Human Solus Tour. Basically, I go around the colonies talking to people and looking at cool stuff." If Moongirl cared she wasn't showing it, she wasn't showing anything. *Solid poker face.* Rick had to ask the question the viewers would ask. And they would want to know about the name. He knew it was a bad idea the moment the words left his mouth. "So, Moongirl? Is that your real name?" Sure enough Moongirl looked annoyed at the question.

"Yes." One word answers made for terrible conversation, and TV, Gary wasn't smiling for once. Rick had to save it. *Back to the dog.*

"So what breed is this handsome pup?" People love talking about their dogs.

"He's a Border Collie German Shepherd mix. And he's three so he's not a pup anymore." This was not going well. Rick needed to find a way to bond with this girl. The whole scene would be cut if there was no chemistry. And she was hot. Rick wanted her on the show.

"So, what brings you to space? Heading anywhere nice?" Rick tried his most charming smile. It did not woo her.

"We're headed back to the Moon. We live there." That got Rick excited.

"That's amazing! You're my first Moonlander!" Rick was genuinely amazed, not Moongirl though... *What excites her?* "What do you do on the Moon?"

"I'm a researcher at the Alien Moon base." *Finally, this shit gets good.* Rick saw Gary smiling in the background.

"Small world! We're doing the next episode there. Tell us about your research." Moongirl perked up. This she would talk about.

"We mostly explore the base, catalogue artefacts, try to decipher markings and reverse engineer technology. Anything that can help us understand where they went and how we can find them." Rick liked this hard-ass-sexy-scientist-alien-hunter.

Moon was passionate about finding aliens, as she iterated several times, it was her life's work. Rick had always been fascinated by the alien disappearance, and he wanted to talk more about it, but Gary was giving him the wrap it up signal. They had long passed the ISS Museum and were nearing the exosphere and ESS. Just about time for one more guest.

"Moon, I want nothing more than to talk about aliens with you but our time is up! How about we continue this conversation next time." Rick turned to the camera. "More on Moongirl's work and aliens next week when we visit the Alien Moon Base!" Rick thanked Moongirl and Gary pushed the new guy into frame.

"This is John Pilg. He's famous too." With that, Gary stepped back.

"John great to have you!" Rick shook John's hand. He had a firm grip.

"Rick good to meet you, finally." Rick was trying to place the name and face. "I've recently become a fan of yours."

"Oh really! Were you not a fan of the show before?" They both laughed.

"Thanks to you aquacyborgs and dolphins are getting councillors. It was a big win for the rights of all living beings." Rick was remembering. He'd seen him on TV during the summer, talking at rallies. Pilg was an anti-war and anti-imperialism journalist. He'd made a documentary about the Mutant Revolution. His passion was starting shit that made trouble for the elite. Pilg had long been a critic of the Council's slow integration of new councillors. He believed the Council should represent all species and all colonies, and do it faster. "I hope you keep up the good work."

"That's the plan!" Rick liked this feeling he got when he did good. *The praise isn't too bad either.* "So, John, what causes are you off to defend now?" Rick was trying to pretend he was on a serious talk show. John was visibly amused.

"Well Rick, I'll be travelling the colonies to shoot the follow up to my documentary Colonation." Rick hadn't seen it. "I'm going to be exploring the colonies to see if there have been any improvements to their lot." Pilg smiled, "in this way we are similar Rick because I like to wing my documentaries."

"Well I can't deny it! I do like to wing it!" Another one of Rick's catchphrases, *and the crowd goes wild.*

Rick needed to get this guy to make a documentary on the Agency. Gary was gesticulating about the arrival or something. Rick got the gist of it. "John it was great to meet you, and hopefully we cross paths again. Very soon." Rick emphasised the "very soon", narrowed his eyes and squeezed Pilg's hand. Hopefully, he'd get the message.

MOONLAND

They'd passed the exosphere and were nearing the ESS. Rick was in space. Earth shrank, and the vast darkness expanded around him. Rick felt something. Something new. He'd heard about that feeling. It was hard to put into words — a sort of primeval pang of nostalgia mixed with the raw realisation of insignificance and a sprinkle of complete awe at life, the Universe and everything. It was a powerful feeling. Perhaps the most powerful he'd ever felt.

They started to slow, Rick sat down and looked up to get a first glimpse of the space station. The cameras were in place to capture his bewilderment, though the lacklustre view somewhat diminished it. Rick could only see the bottom of a black sphere. Amy came to the rescue and projected a hologram of the station for Rick.

"It looks like a snow globe."

"The ESS is an enormous structure. One of six super stations orbiting Terra. Home to thousands and a constant flow of passengers."

"Why?"

"Why what?"

"Why build these stations? Why don't ships just land on Earth?"

"Inertia dampers can't handle the weight of large ships... That's why they still use the elevator for cargo."

Rick turned to the nearest camera bot and made one of

his stupid human faces. "You learn something new every day!"

The space lift docked beneath the station. From there hundreds of cabs and shuttles departed for Moonland. The AI thanked everyone for their custom and wished them well on their journeys. Rick had been busy staring out the window and hadn't noticed Moongirl, Pete and John leave. He'd have liked to stay in touch with them. Hopefully, Amy had noted their AI IDs.

Gary had gotten the bots in place, and they were ready for Rick's exit into the terminal. The shuttle departures were every hour on the hour. They'd just missed one. The team hadn't planned on a visit of the station, but Rick insisted. *Death-Star-space-city, guys?* Under the pretence of being hungry Rick dragged the crew above to look for food. He had Amy locate a place, and they followed her out of the terminal. The stations and all new cities tended to follow the Zero City model. The scale was not the same here, but Rick saw the resemblance. He wondered if they had a pit. Gary was having none of it.

"We're not missing that shuttle, Rick! Let's grab a bite and get out. You can party on the Moon." The cameras were rolling so Rick did some begging and dragging his feet. Didn't want to alienate the fans of drunk Rick.

In the end, they had to get that Moon shuttle. Gary would not relent. *Fucking Gary.* Brock and Amy reassured Rick that this was going to keep happening. Every location he'd visit would blow his mind. Rick thought about that on the shuttle and about whether he should still go ahead with his plan. Maybe he could spend the rest of his life travelling the stars. Play ball. This way he'd see Earth again. He had the suit now perhaps he didn't need enhancements. There was still the brain thing. He might become unscannable. And then death and soul recycling. The end of this life. Back to the Universoul. It all boiled down to whether Rick wanted to die or live longer and die later in an intergalactic war as a hero or something.

The Universe picked that moment to remind Rick of his plan. The armoured suit's bone and tissue stimulation therapy started, and the pain answered the question for him. The shuttle AI informed the passengers that the ship was ready for departure and that artificial gravity would be switched off in a moment. Robot attendants patrolled the aisles, ensuring seatbelts were buckled, and belongings were stored. The moment they were out of sight Rick unbuckled, this was his first real microgravity experience. He wanted to experience it without being tied down. Gary had given the go-ahead. There would be enough time before take-off. Rick floated up out of his seat laughing like a child and swearing this was the best thing ever. Some passengers laughed and others not so much. *Blasés assholes*. Rick performed for his fans and himself. He pretended to swim and rolled and had an excellent few minutes before the attendants put him back in his seat. The commotion swiftly subsided, and the ship resumed its departure countdown.

In his window seat, Rick was back to enjoying the view. He didn't think he could ever get bored of looking at the stars. They'd become rare on Earth. Light pollution blocked out the stars in every Zero City. And, although great achievements of countless benefits, the space stations were bright and they too outshone the starlight. The shuttle ride was quick. Too fast to fit any interviews or interactions. Rick got to enjoy his first real spaceship ride in peace. The kidnapping didn't count.

❖ ❖ ❖

Luna, the Moon, had fascinated people since the dawn of civilisation. Rick was no exception. Currently, Amy was educating him while his face was pressed against the window trying to glimpse the Lunar nation of Moonland.

Moonland was enclosed in a twin magnetic force field. It shielded life from radiation and kept the atmosphere within. Artificial gravity generators set to Earth-g kept people grounded; microgravity was fun, but the long-term effects weren't. Rick would be reminded of that once a day for the foreseeable future when his stimulation modules kicked in.

The lunar population had plateaued at about a million

inhabitants as it mostly served as an R&D world. Luna City was the only city on the Moon, and it was home to scientists and travellers mostly. The outskirts of the city were littered with military bases and research labs. Moonland's tourist appeal had substantially diminished in the decades since its colonisation.

Rick could see Luna City and the shimmering dome that protected it. The shuttle glided indoors through great hangar doors and hovered above its designated landing pad for an instant before setting down. *The space bus has landed.* Passengers were all in a hurry to get off, and Gary signalled Rick to wait. He waited, and while he waited, he peered over the seats, trying to catch a glimpse of Moongirl. He didn't. Maybe she'd travelled some other way.

The spaceport was crowded, and the flow of passengers never ebbed. They'd landed in the Moon shuttle terminal. To their left, Rick spied the cab terminal and private vehicle parking. He was glad they'd taken public transport, he'd never have met Moongirl otherwise.

The group headed straight out of the terminal and towards the train to Luna City. Rick was a bit surprised there wasn't a fanfare waiting for him when he got off the shuttle and again when they exited the terminal. He had walked unimpeded all the way to the train. *Weird.* Rick wasn't sure how he felt about the lack of attention.

"Gary!" Rick reached out and tapped his shoulder. "What's the plan man?"

"We're taking the train to Luna City. Like everyone else."

"Is that it?" Rick tried to hide his disappointment.

"Yeah, we're done for the day." Gary grinned at Rick, "You wanna work some more? Are you OK? Do you have space fever?"

"Fuck you, Gary!"

"Early start tomorrow. Don't stay out too late." Rick had no notion of how much time had passed since their departure from Earth, but maybe it was time for a drink and a bit of night crawling. "Is it night?" Rick asked Amy.

"It is currently night yes. And it will be for the next

thirteen Terran days. Moon days last 708 hours, or 29.5 Terran days." *So it's night then.* Rick's mind drifted to pit thoughts.

"Do they have a pit in Luna City?"

"They do but Rick I should warn you. They might not cater to humans." *No human booze.* Rick didn't believe that for one second. And he could just drink mutant booze. It was stronger, but he'd done it before. It had not ended well.

"Take the camera bots." Gary loved pit footage. Rick didn't like the idea of the camera bots following him all the time. Those clumsy robo-ninjas attracted too much attention.

"I'm not going there for work Gary! I just want a drink and maybe some tail. Don't need everything to be in the show."

"Yes, but everything you say and do is great TV. So the bots follow!" It was pointless arguing more; it would just rouse suspicions. The pits were chaotic places. People got lost in the pits...

The train connected the spaceport to the city centre in a few minutes. First, they passed the farming zone. It was proportionally much larger than the ones on Earth. The farming districts seemed in full production; big machines tended crops as far as the eye could see. Rick had never seen these machines in action. On Earth, the farms mostly served as learning centres. They passed the residential areas and entered the tower district. Rick commented on the puny towers' heights and was told by Amy that structures on Luna couldn't go very high.

"The crust is low density and just a couple of miles deep. Then it's the alien structure's metal." Amy projected a cross section of Luna for Rick and showed him far more than he cared to learn.

The train dropped all its passengers at the Luna exchange. From there people could reach all areas of Moonland. Gary led Rick and the others to another train which would drop them in the hotel district. Which Rick had recently learned was close to the pit district. *It's almost like Gary wants me to drink...* The Luna City pit wasn't dug very deep for the same reasons the towers weren't high. So it wasn't really a pit, more like a big sprawling mishmash of debauchery. It still ticked most of the boxes. As Rick gazed out at the city, he thought the place was a mess, a stunted, dirty version of the Zero Cities of Earth. Not that this was a bad thing. The clean life of Earth hadn't worked out for him, *time to get dirty.*

THE PLOT THICKENS

So far so good. Brock must have thought it a hundred times since they left Terra. They'd arrived at the hotel and checked-in without a single fan bothering them. Brock didn't like unknown environments. He'd been surfing the QI for information, studying the plans and geography of every one of their destinations ahead of their arrival. QI was the internet but in space. The Quantum Entanglement Internet was how Terra stayed in contact with the colonies and more importantly how people could watch Netflix in faraway systems. Brock, like everyone else, was bewildered that it even worked. Even those that had built it were unsure of its exact workings.

Rick had insisted they go looking for a bar the moment they'd dropped their bags. Brock knew where to take him. He'd made the arrangements before even leaving Terra.

Mr T led them through the crowded streets of Luna, *so crowded*. The grim-faced moonlanders paid no attention to them. The upside was no annoying fans. The downside was getting body-checked by every passing person. Not so much a problem for Brock, but Rick had had enough fairly quickly. He'd gotten behind Brock to let him do the shoving. The camera bots were struggling to get in position for their shots. *Good.*

Brock wasn't sure at what point they'd entered the pit. It

only became clear to him when he started noticing scantily clad ladies of the night. *Smooth transition.* Brock knew where to go but was waiting for the opportune time to spirit Rick away.

"Any place that serves human booze?" Brock frowned, Rick was always so impatient.

"Searching the QI now." Amy, annoyingly, was always so helpful.

"I know a place. Follow me." Brock started pushing through the crowd with Rick in tow.

"Hurry up fool." Mr T zoomed ahead, and Amy followed, shouting at him to slow down.

Brock pulled Rick through the crowd. He felt him bounce like a rag doll but didn't slow down. Had to lose those cameras.

"BROCK!"

"What?"

"Stop pulling me! My head is ringing from getting smashed into by all these fucking blind cunts!"

"We're almost there!" Brock pulled Rick into an alley and down some stairs into the underground part of the pit.

They hurried down some dark corridors and pushed through a red door. The place had an old-school arcade vibe. Seventies decoration and eighties neon lights. Video games everywhere. All the classics. Pinball machines, pool tables and ice hockey. The place had an authentic feel to it. Brock instantly loved it, and he knew Rick would too.

"Do they serve humans here?" Rick's face showed wonderment but also worry.

"I had them stock up before we arrived. What do you want?"

"BOOM! You're a legend mate! Whiskey chaser please!" Rick turned to the Space Invaders machine and started playing.

Brock was gone a while, but Rick didn't notice. When he returned, Rick had challenged some guys to Street Fighter XII, and a whole tournament had started. Brock couldn't help but think this must've been the first time Rick was winning a fight.

"Where the fuck have you been? I'm parched from all this

ass-kicking!" Rick executed some vicious flying uppercut move and finished his opponent. "Boom! Next!"

"I was talking to some old friends. I'd like you to meet them."

"What? Now? But I'm kicking some serious ass!" Rick turned back to the game. Everyone was leering and urging him on. He had one eye on the screen, and the other strained to look at Brock. "Mate, can't this wait?"

"Rick this is serious. You can play later."

"Come on fool!" Brock guffawed. Rick must have wished he'd gotten up before Mr T spoke. "That's right fool."

"Get some practice! I'll be back later to kick your asses!" Rick grabbed his drinks, sipped some beer, popped his shot bubble and sipped more beer. "So what's up Brock? Who are these friends of yours?"

"Just follow me." Brock led Rick to the back, through a service door, past the cellar and through a secret wall Brock activated with a series of manoeuvres. The wall slid open revealing a steep staircase that led to a lift. It took them deep beneath the bar and opened onto a dark sloping corridor with lights at the end. Brock led Rick into a large brightly lit room. The light came from the metal surfaces themselves. No fixtures and fittings as far as Brock could tell. "We're here." Furniture had been brought in. The same kind of stuff as in the bar. It looked alien in this immaculate room. Brock nodded at Pops and Jin. Pete was also there. They were sat around a table, looking all serious. Brock looked at Rick. He seemed perplexed.

"What's going on Brock?"

"Rick, these are old friends. I served with them in the Council's special forces a long time ago. Now they help colonists. You've met Pops. He was our commanding officer back in those days. Now he coordinates from Terra." Rick still seemed silenced by confoundment, so Brock continued. "This is Jin, he owns The Arcade Bar above and coordinates on Luna. And you've met Pete, which was unfortunate, fucking Gary. I didn't know Pete was on that elevator. I'd've stopped Gary if I'd known. That was my bad."

"No that was bad comm. All of our faults." Pops' brow deeply furrowed.

"It's my fault. But I had to get out quick. They were onto me." Pete had apparently done some great acting earlier. But if they were onto him already the point was moot.

"Hopefully Pete can complete his mission before they catch up to him." Brock smiled at Rick.

"Not so simple bud."

"None of this is making any sense to me. I'm thankful for the introductions mate, but I have no idea what the fuck you're on about. What the fuck are you all coordinating? What's Pete doing with the dinosaurs?" Brock stayed quiet as Rick scanned the room for a response. Pops met his searching eyes.

"Sit down Rick, and be quiet." Brock pulled out a couple of chairs and Rick took a seat.

"Rick, you have been oblivious to your own life and the happenings of the world around you." Brutal statement but true, Rick stayed quiet. "Confined to an existence dedicated to debauchery you have until recently been uninterested in the lives of people. Not even your own was of concern."

"OK well, that's not very nice." Brock put a quieting hand on Rick's shoulder.

"The reality is that just like your father once did you will have a big part to play in the coming events. This is unfortunate because you're a selfish man and an idiot."

"Did you bring me here to be insulted? 'Cause you could just write hate mail like everyone else..."

"When Brock first made me aware of your desire to challenge the Agency and Council I assumed it was for your own selfish reasons. And it was."

"You know that was a perfect opportunity to say something nice?" Rick shrugged, and Jin cracked a smile, Brock gave him the evil eye. *Don't encourage him.*

"But after your Atlantis episode, we started thinking maybe you had the right stuff. Maybe you could be an asset."

Pops paused, Rick probably wanted to shout at him to come out with it already. Brock was enjoying watching Rick squirm. "There are problems, on Terra and the colonies, issues you seem to have become aware of through your selfish introspection, but you've reached the correct conclusion. The Agency is a problem." Brock knew that would pique Rick's interest. He was probably imagining a ridiculous scenario instead of listening to Pops. "We have reason to believe the production ship that follows your show is tasked with destroying any dissenters identified during the show. We think they'll be targeting Pete as soon as they've reviewed the footage."

"I can tell from the stupid look on your face that you're confused. Now's the time for some questions mate." Brock tried to encourage Rick with a smile.

"What's there to be confused about? The Agency is subverting the system to pit the colonies against each other and Terra." Pops waited for a nod. It didn't come.

Brock took it upon himself to explain a few details to Rick. Food was the root of this problem. Not enough Mr Food stem cell cartridges were exported to the colonies and the company that held the patent and rights wouldn't share the tech. Under advice from the Agency. This was contrary to the vision of the founding Council, but no one did anything about it. Attempts to reverse-engineer Mr Food machines had all failed. The device was magic.

Brock explained that the only available choice for the colonists had been reverting to agriculture to feed their growing populations. Many in the colonies suspected the shortage of Mr Food cartridges was a manufactured lie, which led to unrest, which led to the resistance. The resistance was formed to help the colonies achieve some form of food autonomy. Their goal was to decentralise the production of life-sustaining resources. Stop the us and them rhetoric promoted by the Agency. The inner system produced food and tech and the mid-system produced raw materials and fuel. They needed each other. The resistance mainly carried out industrial espionage. Operating in the shadows trying to acquire technologies that would help bring balance.

"It should all be public domain anyway." Jin was right.

"The colonies just want manufacturing and production independence. Not political independence but it seems this is hard to believe for some paranoid Terrans." Brock continued, but Jin interjected again.

"Anything that benefits civilisation should be shared. It was a core principle of the new world. Your father said that." Brock paused to scowl at Jin and Pops took over.

"The Council fears rebellion. The Agency's media factory has poisoned Terran minds. They are shoring up military presence rather than face the Agency and the real problems they've created." Pops had stood and was approaching Rick. "By advising their clients to create monopolies, they are returning disparity to civilisation. We have ascertained that part of their strategy is discrediting the resistance. And they are planning to achieve this with the use of mercenaries." Brock knew Rick had to ask questions now. He could feel it.

"Right, Brock what the fuck?" *Good first question.* A look of disbelief came across Pops and Pete, and Jin was visibly amused. Brock was not surprised and answered.

"We all served in the the same unit. Pops here fought in the war. Though his war quickly became about finding and protecting us lost kids. He adopted us at different times. Trained us. Made us into the warriors we are today. We started doing dirty work for the Council, bringing "order" and "peace"." Brock had done some questionable things but now was not the time to discuss them. He'd given Rick some air quotes to let him know there was more. But he'd probably missed them, Rick's bemused expression said it all. Brock continued, "I left a little over ten years ago and became a bodyguard. The unit disbanded, and we all went our separate ways. Until a few years ago when Pops started the resistance. I was brought in a few months ago after Atlantis. Things got a little more serious after I joined. An old contact reached out to Pops offering mercenary work. The bad kind."

"They tried to hire us to undermine our own operation!" Brock could tell Pops was seething underneath his composure.

"We believe the corrupt elements of the Council want to use mercenaries to create instability in the colonies and justify a military response. And we know this because they tried to hire Pops." Brock waited to see if Rick had processed everything.

"OK, so you're all super spies and warriors. Explains how you know all you know, I guess. The Agency is poison. We all agree here. And they are corrupting the Council and bringing back the old ways, and starting shit between colonies." Rick stopped, he had that chuffed face Brock hated. "Yeah? OK. And Solus Tour is being used to identify opposition. And mercenaries following us will destroy them and generally cause shit in the name of the resistance. All so there's more war, money and whatever bullshit. Is that about right?"

"Yes." As Brock answered, he saw the features on the others soften.

"OK well, the only thing I don't understand is what Pete's mission is."

"Pete is transporting valuable info to Alpha for reproduction and dissemination."

"What kind of info?"

"Research on how to manipulate stem cells and how to build food cartridges."

"So no dinos?"

"I'm carrying the dinos too. It's my cover."

"It has taken a long time to acquire this data. We've made copies for Brock to carry. Should Pete fail in his mission, we believe Solus Tour would be a great backup team." Pops stopped, and they all waited for Rick's reaction.

"It was my idea, Rick." Brock put a comforting hand on Rick's back. His mind was probably a little blown. Things had escalated substantially.

"So they're going to eat dinosaurs?" There was a long silence, and no one answered. Not what the audience expected, Brock was less surprised.

"Times are hard Rick…" Brock stifled a grin. Pop shot him a disapproving glare.

"Rick they manipulate the cells to create different things. They don't eat dinosaurs." Rick seemed somewhat disappointed by that answer.

"What about Jurassic Park?"

"What about it?"

"Are they building a dino theme park in Proxima or Alpha?

"I don't know… And it's not important bud." Rick thought it was.

"Where are we right now?" Everyone sighed.

"We're in an undiscovered room in the Alien Moon Base, dug beneath Jin's bar. Very far from researchers so unlikely to be discovered any time soon." Rick begged for more information, but Brock was dragging him out. He'd used up everyone's Rick tolerance for one session.

Brock took him back to his Street Fighter tournament and watched him win. Rick seemed happy. It was a nice change.

MOONGIRL

The base was not a tourist location. They had the museum for that. Moon had told her supervisors as much. She was annoyed at having to play tour guide. The base was a serious place for serious people. That was the warning given to Rick when his party had arrived. That fool was swooning all over her again, and she didn't have Moondog to distract him this time.

Moon's team was widely derided around the base. It had been almost a decade since they'd had any results worth sharing. She knew aliens existed. She knew they'd been to Luna and Terra. She just didn't know where they'd gone. And it was her job to find their cosmic address.

Luna was always going to be the first extra-planetary base of operations for the colonisation of the stars. Humanity wanted to mine it and make it a spaceship factory long before they found the alien structure. Moon was part of the team that had discovered the base. She'd called it home since.

They'd discovered the entrance to the base hidden in the shadows of a crater on the dark side of the Moon. It had taken her team years to break in, the first of many frustrations, only to find the base was abandoned, not one soul, not one ship. She was still optimistic then. It was all still very exciting.

Exploration was slow, in twenty years they'd only explored a relatively small portion of the estimated structure. Many secrets still lied concealed within.

Moon wanted to find aliens so bad. If only to say thank you. Though the occupants were gone, they had kindly left the technological treasures that helped accelerate human evolution. She wanted to meet the minds behind such genius. She'd never stop looking. She'd spend a thousand years searching the base if she had to. Maybe she could spare an afternoon for this moronic TV show. Perhaps even educate a few people. Her colleague Antor was currently attempting such a thing.

"Colonisation of the Moon started in the late twenties. Almost immediately after the birth of the first conscious AIs. After the events of the war and purge, it was clear humans needed to spread throughout the stars."

"Always keep backups!" Rick's wisecracks were unrelenting. So far they were not working on Moon. Antor was also unmoved. That annoying Gary guy kept saying it was good TV.

"Officially Luna was abandoned in the seventies because NASA had finished its work there, and the USA had proved itself to be the leader in space exploration. The real reasons were far more interesting..."

Rick cut off Antor with an overly sarcastic tone. "Were they now?" Gary stifled a laugh. *What an idiot.*

Unfazed, Antor continued, "when the truth was released it showed that time and time again the Apollo astronauts were warned away from Luna by advanced aliens." Back then it had really captured people's imaginations, took their minds off the lingering memories of the purge and gave them hope in something bigger than themselves. Antor waited for Rick's comment, but it never came, so he resumed his lecture. "Almost as soon as construction began the colonists noticed the impenetrable metal sphere below the surface. The matter displacement drill had to be invented to breach the alien doors. Though not before trying and failing with every drilling method in existence.

"That's what she said!" Moon shook her head. *Did Antor set him up?*

"Good one Mr Archer." *No Antor what have you done? Why*

encourage him?

Rick would be coming after her now. Moon just knew it. Antor signalled her. Time to talk.

"The first thing we found when we breached the base were neatly stacked stargate kits."

"What they were just lying there?"

"No, they were neatly stacked in between the entrance and what we identified as a hanger." Moon waited a few seconds in case Rick had more on his mind. "Initially nobody knew what they were, but after a few hundred years in virtual research Luna's brightest were able to reverse-engineer the devices and create the nanobot stargate kits."

They passed the kit room and found themselves in a vast hangar, devoid of any ships just like on the first day. Though, as Moon explained, tools and parts had been left behind and that had kept scientist busy. As they crossed the vast room, Antor regaled them with his theories on the alien disappearance.

"Perhaps recent times' most exciting and simultaneously frustrating discovery was that of alien civilisations. Or should I say traces of civilisations? It is clear this place was built by an advanced group of beings that just picked up and left one day…"

"Just like your daddy!" Rick put on an accent that made Brock frown. Gary thought it was great though and the slightest smile appeared in the corner of Antor's synthetic mouth before it opened to resume. Moon liked that joke least of all.

"As I was saying, the base was empty though exceptional gifts were left behind. The stargate kits and the mutating metal used to build the base, once understood, considerably improved our capacity for space engineering. Effectively this base's discoveries transformed us into Homo Cyberneticus Cosmicus." Antor wasn't done, but Rick interjected.

"Not me! No-Homo…" Rick paused a moment, "Cyberneticus…" Rick had probably wanted to make a better joke, but halfway through it seems he got sad. Moon had not seen this expression on his face before.

"Do not despair Mr Archer! You are most definitely Homo Cosmicus, and many ancient philosophers would argue that you are actually Cyberneticus because of your suit. The tech may not be inside of you, but it is very much a part of you."

Moon saw the light in Rick's eyes, and she felt sorry for him. Suddenly and all at once she understood his plight. He was a sad man — a clown who kept no smiles for himself.

Antor waited for Rick to say something, but when nothing came, Moon decided to pick up the lecture. "Since our ascent to space-faring species we have been sending ships to promising systems trying to find aliens and setting up colonies. Though so far no aliens have been found." Moon stopped. Rick looked like he had a question.

"So what happened to the aliens?" Rick asked the question because he had to. But the answer was common knowledge.

"The running theory is that aliens left when the war started. They all abandoned their missions and returned to their respective home worlds. They probably didn't think humans would survive another big war." Moon's eyes fell to the ground. It was so frustrating, *why couldn't they wait a little longer?*

They'd reached the end of the hangar and exited through a corridor lined with rooms set up as labs. Moon led them to her office.

Moon practically lived in that office. Her typical day involved waking up with her dog. Her only friend. They'd usually eat breakfast in her dorm room near the base. Her mornings mostly involved looking over notes and talking with her colleagues about their lack of progress. As an ancient language expert and astronomer, her job involved studying artefacts and any data that might hold answers as to where everyone had gone, as she was currently explaining to Rick and the camera bots. Progress was non-existent for her team. Moon stood by her desk. She glanced at the holopads and alien objects that cluttered it, suddenly conscious that she might appear messy on TV. Smartscreens and more artefacts of varying sizes and shapes lined the walls. This room probably looked cluttered to the uninitiated. It was in fact very well organised... To her.

"We need to find something like a Rosetta stone." Moon had studied hundreds of objects, and many of them seemed to have completely different sets of symbols. "So far the only thing we've achieved is the identification of twelve different sets of markings, twelve languages, twelve different alien species." This had taken them many years, and she initially thought it was a decent achievement. "But we don't know much about what they're saying..."

"What like nothing at all?" Rick blurted the question out. He felt bad the moment he did.

"Don't sell yourself short, Moon! Your team has identified the ON button in twelve alien languages!" Antor laughed, Moon heard laughter down the corridor. *Dicks.*

Moon had become deflated about the quest for alien civilisations. Much to her annoyance Antor's team had made giant leaps for transhumankind. His team discovered and reverse-engineered dozens of artefacts a year. And they regularly brought new items for her to analyse and catalogue. The more they explored, the more objects piled up in her lab. Adding more questions and answering none.

Antor had started leading the group deeper in the base while regaling them with his team's achievements. "Our researchers are constantly going further in the base, breaking through new doors and opening up new sections to explore. Unfortunately, no instruction manuals come attached!" Antor laughed and turned towards Moon. "Our work would be impossible without teams like Moon's. These scientists, ancient alien theorists, advanced technologists and linguistics specialists work tirelessly to help us understand these artefacts." Moon smiled, that was nice to say, especially on TV. "It is taxing work, and sadly no discovery has matched that of the first. The discovery of the stargate kits and reverse engineering of portal technology brought about the single most important advancement. It made us into a spacefaring species."

"Fuck yeah!" Rick pumped his fist and bowed his head,

and in a moment of, what Gary called pure TV gold, Antor did the same. Moon shook her head annoyed at how much fun they were having. *This is a serious place.*

"Fuck yeah!" Antor's synthetic voice echoed Rick's.

Antor had led them to the universal map room. Researchers studied a large three-dimensional interactive holo-map of the known Universe. Astronomers kept the map updated with data from satellites, probes, telescopes and colonies. Moon had sworn to herself that one day she'd mark the location of an alien homeworld on that map. *One day.*

Antor was still droning on, but all eyes were on the holo-map. Moon had taken control and zoomed in on Terra.

"Shortly after the colonisation of Luna and the creation of Moonland, nanobots fleets began their trips to the closest systems. The Alpha Centauri system was top of the list." Moon pulled away from Terra so that only Solus and Alpha were visible. "Soon afterwards more nanobot fleets were sent to Tau Ceti, Wolf and every likely planet-supporting system within forty light years of Solus."

Moon had them mesmerised. Their eyes followed the lines that showed the fleets' journeys through the stars. Space is really big. This map was great at showing that.

"Billions of nanobots were assembled and programmed to re-assemble themselves as stargates upon arrival."

Moon brought the nanobot ships schematics just above Rick's head. She nodded in approval at his suitably awed expression before these infinitely complex machines. Thousands of them assembled into ships no bigger than a pack of smokes. And millions of these mini ships formed great fleets that moved in unison like bird flocks through the vast emptiness. Made of a wondrous programmable metal that could shapeshift to match external conditions and absorb and produce some energy; the same mutating metal as the base and most artefacts. The ships' diamond nuclear batteries powered onboard miniature lasers that fired almost continuously at their sapphire light sails. It was the best system until the advent of the fusion drive.

"The first wave of nanobots was able to reach near the speed of light by the time they exited the heliosphere, in less than five years the first stargates were operational and people ventured into a new star system. Alpha."

Antor stopped. This bit was always a bummer. The atmosphere had been electrifying. The whole system had turned into one big party as everyone awaited first contact. Moon remembered being so excited then, the world had held its breath together. All expected the discovery of an advanced civilisation. People waiting for humanity's children, enthused at the idea of sharing knowledge and culture. That was not to be the case. The Alpha system was not home to any civilisations. When the stargates opened for Tau Ceti, Wolf, Eridani and the Glieses' researchers and pundits alike believed this time alien cultures would be waiting. They were not.

"How could six systems with dozens of planets and moons between them not have civilised life on them?" It's the question the fans would ask, or so Gary told Rick. Moon had an answer ready.

"Many now think the alien visitors came from much farther away, too far for us to reach with current technology. The search, so far, has been conducted in places we can reach, but many say the search should focus on places mentioned by ancient civilisations." Moon drew attention to the map and zoomed in on Orion's belt. "The stars in Orion have been suggested as candidates for a mission. But distances are more than ten times greater than anything current ships have travelled. Public support for search and expansion missions has waned, people and resources are spread thin." Gary was telling Rick it wasn't such a great idea to end the tour on such a downer. Moon scowled at him; *science is not entertainment.*

"So what's next?" Rick and the viewers wanted some hope. Moon glanced at Antor; he would probably disappoint. Moon would give them a glimmer.

"We continue our work and hope for a breakthrough." Rick was overtly disappointed with that answer. "Technology is advancing rapidly. We will find them eventually. I am sure of this." That was as positive a note as they'd get from her.

THIRD TIME LUCKY

Luna Park was fun, but not that fun. Rick was disappointed. Many of the rides delivered an inferior rush because of the diminished gravity. Apart from the catapult. Getting flung into space inside that tiny sphere had been exhilarating even if the way down was less intense. The bouncing castle maze and assault courses looked like fun at first, but the laughing children infestation put a damper on the experience. Rick had realised too late that every surface was sticky with child filth, a composite of burst sugary bubbles, chocolate-like smears and dribble coated every surface of this otherwise fun experience. Rick soldiered on through the sticky bouncing children hellscape, crushing children under his weight every time he fell was the highlight of the experience.

Once that ordeal was cleared he was apprehensive about any more rides, but Gary had insisted they make the most of the theme park. The viewers wanted to see more. *Fucking Gary.* Rick put his armoured suit back on and pleaded with Gary.

"Mate, do we really have to go on with this crap?" Gary frowned. The cameras were rolling, and Luna Park was an Agency client. Rick didn't care. "I'm not taking the suit off anymore."

"I don't know what was in your food today, but you need to chill the fuck out." Gary's tone surprised Rick. "We have work to do, and you're the one who wanted Luna Park in the first place."

"I didn't think there would be so many children..." The problem was not the park.

"What did you expect mate? It's a fucking theme park!" Gary seemed relaxed.

"Yeah, but I thought it was an adult theme park, kinda like Paris."

"Why would you think that? What's wrong with you?" They were all laughing at him now. This is why people loved the show. He simply couldn't escape his fate.

"I thought the Moon only had scientists and soldiers on it." Rick thought his logic was sound.

"And they can't have children? And what about tourists?" Rick felt stupid. "Let's just do the buggy safari to the original Moon landing spot. Then we'll call it. Fair?"

Rick begrudgingly accepted the deal, and they did the safari. On the upside, there were no children in sight. Probably because the ride was boring, if they'd just let the buggies go a little faster it could have been fun. But they didn't. So it wasn't. The original Moon landing spot was unchanged since sixty-nine and was underwhelming as Rick had iterated several times. Gary must have agreed because he didn't make them linger in the park after that.

Rick sat at the front of the train on the ride back to the city and it was a better rush than any of the shitty rides in the park. He would need to get slightly drunk now, to aid with the assimilation of his second day in space. This time the camera bots would follow him. As would Gary, he had said so several times on the train to make sure it was clear to Rick. *It's fucking clear dickhead.*

◆ ◆ ◆

Back in the crowded streets of Luna city Rick followed Amy, and the others followed Rick. The Moonland shoot was pretty much done, tomorrow they'd board the Solus Express to Mars. The camera bots had a little more b roll to capture, and they could do so while the team wandered the city looking for a drinking hole. The group entered one of the city's busy plazas, and Amy and Mr T floated on ahead to find a suitable bar before an increasingly frustrated Rick went on one of his rants, then he spotted Moongirl in the crowd. She was walking towards them with the dog in tow. His heart lifted the moment he saw her. *Third time lucky*. She seemed deep in thought and didn't notice Rick approach her.

"Good evening, Moon!" Rick tried a little bow to add to his humorous charm. She snapped out of her musings startled.

"Oh! Hey, sorry didn't see you." Moondog came up to Rick begging for attention. Rick wished Moongirl was a bit more like Moondog. Though maybe it'd be weird if Moongirl walked up to him and started licking his hand. *Maybe*.

"I'm so glad we bumped into you! I didn't get a chance to thank you earlier. I really enjoyed the tour of the base. It was a childhood dream come true." Rick was genuine, but his smarmy reputation probably ruined his attempts at being earnest.

"Just doing my job." If there was a vaccine for Rick's charm, Moon had taken it.

The conversation was not going very well. The awkwardness was palpable, and any minute now Gary would intervene. Then Pete ran into the background. Moondog perked up, and his body went rigid. Moon pointed in Pete's direction. "Wasn't that guy on your show?"

Pete seemed to be in a hurry. Rick looked at Brock. He knew that face, that was the "oh shit face". Pete was pushing past the crowd when he noticed them. It was hard not to see Brock. He towered above most people, and his green Mohawk was famous. Pete made a beeline for them. He was carrying a backpack that he unshouldered and held against his chest as he body-slammed anyone in his way. Gary and everyone else in the area had now noticed the commotion. Pissed-off people were picking themselves up off the ground and turning to shout abuse at Pete who powered through the crowd towards Brock. The cameras were rolling and were about to capture Pete make contact. *Not good.*

Moondog looked up and barked. He'd heard the soft hum of the ship first. It had no markings to identify it as Council or anyone else for that matter. Rick thought it looked a lot like their production ship. If Amy had been around, she could have confirmed his suspicions, but she wasn't. She'd be off looking for booze when he died, poetic.

Luna City was a no-fly zone, so it was only a matter of minutes before security bots showed up to give pursuit, but it only took a second to shoot. A salvo of plasma fire was unleashed onto Pete's position before the ship vanished. The explosions threw dozens of people, including Rick and the others. Smoke and fire filled the plaza — those who could, fled.

Rick was sprawled on the ground, dazed, ears ringing, shouting at Mom to switch to thermal imaging or something. If it hadn't been for the suit, Rick would have probably died. Beeping and red flashing on his HUD made him aware of that fact. Mom quickly got everything under control. The display started showing waypoints and IDs. Rick could see Moon a dozen metres away, hunched over Moondog. Gary was checking on the camera bots, one of them was down. Half its body melted by the hot plasma and its systems fried by the ionised particles. Gary was fiddling with the head. Probably trying to save the footage. *Priorities Gary, priorities.* Brock was moving towards Pete who was also down.

The smoke had begun to clear a bit. Rick switched back to normal vision and saw that Pete was fairly hurt, his legs were missing. He pressed his pack onto Brock's chest. Rick couldn't make out what they were saying, so he edged closer. The cracking of railgun and plasma fire started from a side street and Brock shouted at Rick to get down. Superheated projectiles sped through the air leaving blazing trails and arcing electricity behind them. The ground and walls erupted around Rick. Smoke and flames filled the plaza again. Rick could here pings on his suit from where shrapnel was ricocheting off him. The beeping and red flashing started again. *Fuck this shit.*

"Mom! I want to shoot back! Fucking do what you have to, but I'm standing up and shooting down that street in one second." Rick looked at his wrists. The plasma cannons started glowing. "How does it work?"

"Just aim and think shoot." *Nice and straightforward,* Rick liked that. He remembered Pops saying something about the genius brainwave interface the dolphins had built. "So simple a moron could use it", *thanks Bubbles.* He raced towards an overturned vending machine near the hostile street's mouth. Brock was shouting obscenities at him, but he stood up from behind his cover anyway, raised both his fists and unleashed. Rick's arms shook as fireballs shot out of his wrist cannons. He was surprised by the recoil, but the suit absorbed much of the force and Rick only shot off target a few times.

Fiery explosions engulfed the end of the street. The incoming fire stopped. Rick rushed over to Moon. She was alright — a few cuts and bruises. Moondog was hurt. Tears streamed down the side of her dusty face. Rick's helmet started ringing, Amy's name was flashing on his display. Rick picked up the incoming call.

"Rick are you OK? Where are you? What's happening? We're trying to get back to you, but streets are sealed off. Security bots are saying there was a terrorist attack." Amy was talking too fast. Too much was going on for Rick.

"Just get back to us." Rick hung up and turned back to Moon. She was crying and close to catatonic. Smoke had filled the street again, and he couldn't see Brock or Gary anymore. "Mom, waypoints." Instantly the information came up on the HUD. Pete had gone cold. *Dead. Fuck.* Brock was speed-crawling towards them when the incoming fire started again.

"We need to get the fuck out of here." Brock was over Rick and the Moons now. He scanned the area waiting for the attack to relent. "OK, let's move. Rick take Moon. I have the dog. Let's go. Head towards Gary. Go, go, go!" Brock gently picked up the dog and Rick grabbed Moon's blood-soaked hand.

Gary didn't seem panicked at all. He appeared entirely

focused on saving the bot's head. His Smartcube floated around him blocking shrapnel. Rick had respect for that kind of commitment. However crazy it was. Brock grabbed Gary by the collar and kept going. Gary wouldn't let go of the bot's head, so Brock tore it off and handed it to him. "Move, move, move. Don't stop running!" They got off the plaza and turned a couple of corners and caught their breath for a second. "We have to keep moving." Everyone started to shout different things at Brock, but he was urging them on again. Rick knew it was pointless when Brock was in soldier mode.

BROCK MOTHERFUCKIN' DYNAMITE

The shell-shocked group met Amy and Mr T as they entered the hotel lobby. Brock hurried everyone to Rick's room. It took a little while for everyone to come out of their stupor but when they did; questions started firing in every direction. Brock was administering first aid to the dog. Moongirl was crying and begging him.

"Please, please, please. Don't let my baby die. Please save him. Please, I beg you. Please…"

Brock didn't respond. It should have been obvious just by watching him that he was doing his best. It had been a while since he'd had to dress a wound. And he'd never done it on a dog. He'd field dressed the Turk once. The hairiest guy Brock had ever seen. He'd shaved him. He needed to shave the dog.

Moon started screaming when he pulled his blade out. Crystal-shattering. Thankfully it went back to begging immediately after.

"I'm not gonna hurt your dog, but I do need to shave him if I'm going to save him."

Surprisingly enough Rick didn't make a joke. The severity of the situation was not lost on him. He was maturing…

The blade was sharp, and Brock expertly removed bloodied clumps of hair while Moon held the dog's head and whispered sweet words. Shrapnel. Burning hot chunks of twisted metal. The dog had three embedded in his left leg and lower back. No vital organs were hit. But those things had to come out before the dog bled out. Brock had Mr T scan the dog to locate the exact position of the shrapnel. Mr T then activated his tractor beam and positioned himself in line with the entry angle. Slowly he pulled out the projectiles. The dog howled and struggled, then settled on whimpering. The things were still hot. Brock closed the wounds and bandaged the dog. He gave it some painkillers and laid it on the bed.

Brock stretched and took a look around the room. Gary was checking the camera bots, and Rick was looking out the window. Brock went over to the holoscreen and switched to the news. The official story was a terrorist group had attacked the Last Human TV crew.

"This is crazy! Why would terrorists attack us! We're only making TV!" Gary was pacing up and down the room. Brock was shaking his head at Rick. *No, say nothing.* Gary was still raving on hysterically. "If anything we're trying to help the colonies. It makes no sense..." Gary turned back to his camera bots. "This makes no sense. I need to review the footage..." He was about to start syncing with the holoscreen when Dave burst through the door.

"What the actual fuck!" The question didn't seem directed at anyone in particular.

"We don't know! We were literally just interviewing Moongirl when this ship just opened fire on us!" Rick was going with the TV story. *Good.*

"Why did you return fire? You're not security forces or some fucking superhero. We don't have insurance for this kind of bullshit. There is security drone footage of you shooting fireballs like a blind idiot. You've damaged several buildings, injured bystanders and you killed someone." *Killed someone.* Brock's heart sank. *Shit just got real.* He could see the darkening look on Rick's face. Gary must have seen it too because he intervened to stop the spiralling.

"If it weren't for Rick we would've all died. We didn't have enough Smartcubes to shield us…"

"Shut the fuck up Gary!" Dave snapped at Gary and turned his attention back to Rick who was staring at the floor in disbelief.

"Did I really kill someone?" Brock knew Rick. He wasn't the type to want to kill someone. But then he thought most people probably didn't think they'd kill someone until they did. *Shit happens and then you die.*

"Yes." Dave's anger was simmering now.

"Wow…" Rick stood there dumbfounded.

Brock had seen it. Rick hadn't aimed or known what he was doing. This was nothing. Strangling someone. Or stabbing them. That leaves a more profound mark on the soul.

"Was he one of the attackers?"

"Yes." Dave's answer immediately lifted everyone's spirits.

"Well fuck him then." Dave did not like that.

"No fuck you, Rick. You've jeopardised the show."

"No fuck you, Dave! Those fuckers who attacked us jeopardised the show!" Dave smiled a slight smile, an evil smile. Brock saw it.

"Well you need to condemn the resistance and their terrorist actions in the next episode, and you need to go on the Moonland news to do it as well." *There it is.*

"Shut the fuck up Dave! We'll do what we have to, but now is not the time for your bullshit. So why don't you fuck off and do your job and sort out this PR shitstorm." Dave tried to hold Brock's menacing glare for a few instants, but he couldn't for very long. *Nobody can. I'm Brock Motherfuckin' Dynamite.*

"Enough fuckery!" And with that Dave left. Everybody seemed to breathe easier once he'd gone. That asshole could suck the fun out a party through a mile-long silly-straw.

Amy and Mr T had just finished syncing with everyone.

They were up to speed. Brock was thinking about what to do with Moon and Gary. Moongirl would be a target now. The heavy-handed mercenaries hired by the Agency were dangerously careless. And Gary... It seemed Gary was not in league with Dick and Dave. Everyone was looking around the room, someone was about to speak. It was Amy.

"Right, your attention please." Gary stopped pacing, Moongirl looked up but stayed on the bed cradling Moondog, Rick turned to Amy, and Brock sighed and took a seat. "Mr T and I have analysed the situation, and it is not good. Gary, Moongirl, we're sorry you got dragged into this. But this is the reality. The people who attacked Pete will attack again. Everyone that interacts with Rick is a target. That means you, Moon. According to our predictions, you will most likely be the next target." Moongirl started protesting but was cut off by Mr T.

"Listen up fool!" Mr T cranked up the volume on the holo-screen. The news anchor's voice filled the room.

"Among the casualties in the Luna City attack was the great journalist John Pilg. His body was found..." The voice dimmed as the volume went down. Mr T was satisfied he'd made his point.

"No, no, no, no, no, no!" Moon went up to Rick. Brock could recognise mounting hysteria when he saw it. *Just weather the storm Rick.* "What is happening? What is this? Is this part of your show? Is this a joke?" She marched over to Gary, "these cameras are filming right? This is all part of the show right?" Moon was pleading now. Black tears streamed down her cheeks.

"Listen to me, Moon." Rick walked up to Moongirl and brought her in for a hug. She sobbed as he spoke softly. "Your dream is to find aliens. Right?" That slowed her crying. "There is no reason your dream has to change." She looked up at him with her teary eyes, and in that instant, Rick looked like he was in love. *Fuck.* "You have to come with us. We'll keep you safe." Moon didn't seem convinced. Her body language was saying no, but she didn't break away from the embrace. "You can't stay here. You have to take your dream on the road. Like I did. People are trying to kill you now."

"But I haven't done anything wrong. I'm just a researcher." Now Moon moved away from Rick and looked around the room pleadingly.

"I'm sorry Moon. You can't go back to your old life. They will kill you before you can explain your position. You saw it with your own eyes." Amy floated closer to Moon and tried the feeling sorry emoji face on her display.

"They didn't attempt to make contact. They opened fire at a distance..." Brock's voice trailed off as he thought back on the attack, "savages..."

"I've always wanted to find aliens. So how about this? Let's find aliens together." Then in a stroke of madness, Rick went over to one of the camera bots, Steve was his name, and squared up to the lens. "You hear that? The Last Human is going to find aliens! We're going interstellar!" Brock was signalling Gary to stop recording.

"What the fuck Rick?" Brock hoped Rick would understand this was a question from the inflexion at the end.

"What?" He hated when Rick did that.

"What do you mean what? What the fuck are you doing?"

"Simple. We honour Pete's mission and John Pilg's and Moon's. We find aliens, we deliver Pete's package, and we report on the situation on the colonies."

"That won't work Rick! Everything we record gets beamed to the support ship, and we'll get censored." Gary had something to say about that. Brock could feel things escalating again.

"Not anymore!" Gary was up, pacing again, he was getting excited. It looked like he'd just snorted a fat line of marching powder. "I'm in! Let's fucking go guerrilla. Let's shoot the greatest show ever! We can handle everything ourselves and just beam a finished product straight to Terra. They'll have to air it. Or we just air it ourselves on Youtube. They can't control us! They can't stop us!" Gary started laughing. Probably his nerves.

Rick told Steve to start recording again. "Alright fans!

Things are getting crazy up in here! We can't trust anyone, so we're going dark! But tune in for live videos and new episodes of Solus Tour: Off The Reservation! Shot guerrilla-style while pursued by vicious mercenaries. Did I hear anyone say BEST SHOW EVER!" Brock still wasn't convinced and he told Rick that much. "Mate, this is the only way, the fans will protect us. If we don't keep the cameras rolling, we'll die a lot faster. Amy tell him this is a good plan."

"Brock, Rick is right, keeping the show going will make it harder for people to attack us. It is completely unexpected and will put off our true enemy." Brock hadn't thought of keeping Gary around and the show rolling. This could actually work. *Sometimes stupid ideas are the best ideas.* He hated that he'd just had that Rick-thought.

"We'll see won't we." Brock was on board.

"Moon?" Brock could tell Rick was really hoping she'd come with them.

"Well, it's not like I have a choice. But Moondog is coming too. Also, we need to get my Smartcube before we leave." No one had said anything, but Brock had found it weird that Moon didn't have a cube.

"I wondered about that." Rick too apparently.

"Yeah she's quite independent, but we're neural-linked. She always knows where I am and what I'm doing. She's freaking out right now."

"OK, we get the cube, and then we get off Moonland." Nods from everyone. "Oh, and nobody says anything to that prick Dave." Brock was pleased he'd seen the last of Dave.

❖ ❖ ❖

The next hour was spent re-organising their schedule. As far as Moon, Gary and the camera bots knew they were being pursued by some militant terrorists; and it was probably best to keep it that way for the time being. They were booked on a Solus Express to Mars City for the next Terran morning, but

Brock wanted them to leave as early as possible. Gary tried to argue that that wouldn't sit well with Dave. He'd told Gary that Dave could go fuck himself and to upload some clips to the show's Youtube channel. Once the fans were on board, and they went viral Dave would be powerless to stop them. Gary was swayed by that. The power of the fans should never be underestimated. He'd gotten to work immediately. Moon had gone back to her dog. Brock pulled Rick aside while everyone busied themselves.

"Rick don't fuck everything up because of a woman!" Brock paused, no reaction from Rick. "Don't wanna burst your bubble but you realise love is just pheromones producing a chemical reaction that compels living things to reproduce to further their genetic code." Brock stopped. Rick was smiling.

"That was hot! You're making me hard! Talk sweet to me some more handsome." Rick burst out laughing. Brock wanted to concuss him. "Listen mate, this is a good plan. And Moon coming with us is just... It's just a happy coincidence."

"Or unhappy if you ask her."

"She was in a rut. She said so herself. A bit of adventure is vivifying." Rick was beaming. Brock sighed. A happy Rick was far more annoying than the usual drunk or depressed Rick. "You know they'd kill her. I'm not lying." Brock shrugged, Rick was right. They'd tie up all loose ends. No point in arguing with Rick when he was like that.

They left in a hurry, Brock had meant to let them pack but his instincts screamed at him to make haste. The hotel checkout happened without any incidents. Brock was real nervous the whole time Amy was at the counter. He was carrying Moondog in a blanket. The dog was stable but would need surgery. Moongirl was right by him, petting her dog and murmuring loving nonsense. Rick was by the door scanning the street.

Everyone was on edge, but the walk to the train station and journey to the space station went smoothly. Still, no time to relax. They headed straight to the Solus Express terminal. Just as Brock was wondering how they'd ever find Moon's Smartcube the little fucker appeared.

"Mom!" *Mom?* The cube came up to Moon, and they touched faces. *Interesting greeting.* Brock shot a glance at Mr T who noticed and came on the neural link immediately.

"Don't you think about it fool!"

Moon turned to the others and introduced the crew to her AI. "Mom, this is the Last Human, Rick, his bodyguard Brock and their AIs Amy and Mr T." Moon waved at Gary and the camera bots. "That's the director, his AI and the camera bots. Not sure what they're all called." Moon's AI floated around saying hi to everyone. When she stopped in front of Brock, he saw that she didn't use emojis on her display. Instead, there was a flawless 3D model of someone's human face. It looked like someone's head in a box. He wondered if he should do the same with Mr T. It was a bit weird.

"How do you change the display from emojis to a 3D model of a face?" That was not the question the others were expecting. This was one of those things everybody knew, but Rick had never bothered to inquire about. Amy answered.

"You have to pay a licensing fee for celebrity faces. Quite exorbitant. But if you use a relative's, it's free." Rick turned to Moon.

"Yes. My Smartcube AI is my mother." Moon got the answer out before Rick could formulate the question.

Brock put a stop to the conversation and gestured at the group to get moving. He was leading them towards the terminal when Moondog started whimpering. The dog felt the danger before his advanced sensors. Brock stopped. Amy and Mr T ascended to get an overview. The Solus Express terminal was one section over but the giant gateway that separated the parts made for a perfect ambush point, both walls were lined with mercs, Brock knew it. It was hard not to notice the fewer people around them. The flow was being ebbed somewhere. Rick called Gary over, he could tell something was up.

"I want you to start a live feed. I want the fans to see us board the Solus Express live." Gary didn't question it. He gave

Rick a thumbs up when they were live. "OK, Brock. We are live. The fans are watching us. What's going on?" Rick paused and looked at Steve's lens face, they both turned to Brock. *I'll play your game you lunatic.*

"We suspect the mercenary terrorists from earlier are going to try to stop us from boarding the Solus Express." Rick was nodding like he could hear music. "But we are boarding that ship or my name isn't Brock Dynamite."

"Fuck yeah!" Steve turned back to Rick. "You heard the man. Shit is about to get real! Hold on to your seats." Brock handed the dog to Moon and grabbed Rick by the shoulders.

"Rick this is real! You understand that, right?" Rick nodded. "OK, I'm going to take care of those punks. Amy and Mr T will back me up. Moon, Rick you run for the Solus Express. Gary and the camera bots too. You don't fucking stop. You don't fucking fight. You get aboard the fucking ship. Clear?" Everyone nodded yes. Rick was slower to nod and that worried Brock.

There were very few people left now. The mercs had learnt from their last experience. Amy and Mr T had received the instructions from Brock. The cameras were rolling, and the fans were watching. Millions were tuning in.

The Smartcubes dashed through the massive gates and were instantly fired upon. The cubes didn't have much offensive capabilities, they weren't weapons, but they made for great distractions. Their fast recharging shields made them perfect for protecting people from incoming fire, or drawing it away. Brock was conscious a direct hit from shield-busting ammo would destroy the AIs, but he trusted them to dodge. Which so far they were doing admirably.

Brock sped towards the gateway, and two large pistols jumped out of his thigh compartments and into his hands. Without slowing, Brock screw-jumped into the next section unleashing death. He counted six enemies on each side. Now two on the right and four on the left. He landed with a forward roll and spun around shooting. Rick and the others were coming through. The mercs were still shooting at Amy, and Mr T.

Brock had finished the last two on the right and was charging the guys on the left. They had just shifted their attention to him. *Too late.* He quickly had the situation under control and started jogging after the others. Rick had hung back to watch him fight and gave him a thumbs up before turning to join the others. In the next section, people seemed to be going about their regular business. *Almost clear.*

A second team was waiting in ambush. Moon and Gary's AIs were able to block some of the incoming fire. Rick wasn't close enough. He went down like a sack of potatoes.

Brock opened fire as he ran towards Rick. He shouted at everyone to get down. "Fuck, fuck, fuck, Rick, don't you fucking die on me, not after you started all this shit." *Don't you fucking dare.*

To be continued in:
The Last Human: Space Shenanigans

AFTERWORD

Why are you still reading? The book is over. Is it because you liked it? Do you want more? You can probably get your hands on Book 2 right now, if you're in the right time and space head on over to Amazon and pick up a copy.

If not, you could always head over to my blog and read some more of my nonsense there. The first post is about writing and the second editing, maybe you'll find them interesting, educational or even funny, maybe not. If you want to find out about why I write and my process head over to www.thelasthuman.co/blog

If you liked the book leaving a good review would do wonders for my ego. Telling people about how it changed your life and that they should order it right now would also be great.

If you made it this far, thank you for taking the time to read The Last Human. Rick and friends will be back in Space Shenanigans!

Printed by Amazon Italia Logistica S.r.l.
Torrazza Piemonte (TO), Italy